PRAISE FOR MIS

"Funny, charming, and rebellious. I can't wait to see what happens next!"

—James Riley, *New York Times* bestselling author of the Story Thieves series and the Revenge of Magic series

"A cliff-hanger ending will leave readers eagerly awaiting the next installment."

—*Booklist*

PRAISE FOR JEN CALONITA'S FAIRY TALE REFORM SCHOOL SERIES

"This fast-paced mash-up of fairy tales successfully tackles real-life issues such as prejudice, gender-role conformity, and self-esteem… More adventures are to come for Gilly."

—*Kirkus Reviews* on *Switched*

"Mermaids, fairies, trolls, and princesses abound in this creative mash-up of the Grimms' most famous characters. This whimsical tale is a surprising mixture of fable, fantasy, and true coming-of-age novel."

—*Kirkus Reviews* on *Tricked*

"Fairy Tale Reform School is spellbinding and wickedly clever. Gilly is smart, spunky, and a hilarious narrator, and I cannot wait to read about her next adventure!"

—Leslie Margolis, author of the Annabelle Unleashed novels and the Maggie Brooklyn mysteries on *Flunked*

"Fairy Tale Reform School is a fresh and funny take on the enchanted world. (And who hasn't always wanted to know what happened to Cinderella's stepmother?)"

—Julia DeVillers, author of the Trading Faces identical twin series and *Emma Emmets, Playground Matchmaker* on *Flunked*

"This clever novel and its smart, endearing cast of characters will have readers enchanted and eager for the implied sequel(s)."

—*Bulletin of the Center for Children's Books* on *Flunked*

"Gilly's plucky spirit and determination to oust the culprit will make *Flunked* a popular choice for tweens."

—*School Library Journal* on *Flunked*

"There's much to amuse and entertain fans of classic tales with a twist."

—*Booklist* on *Flunked*

Also by Jen Calonita

Royal Academy Rebels
Misfits
Outlaws

Fairy Tale Reform School
Flunked
Charmed
Tricked
Switched
Wished

ROYAL ACADEMY
REBELS

MISFITS

JEN CALONITA

sourcebooks
young readers

Published by Sourcebooks Young Readers, an imprint of Sourcebooks Kids
P.O. Box 4410, Naperville, Illinois 60567-4410
(630) 961-3900
sourcebookskids.com

The Library of Congress has cataloged the hardcover edition as follows:

Names: Calonita, Jen, author.
Title: Misfits : Royal Academy rebels / Jen Calonita.
Description: Naperville, Illinois : Sourcebooks Jabberwocky, [2018] |
    Summary: Forced to attend Enchantasia's Royal Academy, Devin teams up with
    other misfits to investigate why Olivina, the fairy godmother/headmistress, is
    obsessed with villains rather than teaching them to be proper princes and princesses.
Identifiers: LCCN 2018010618 | (hardcover : alk. paper)
Subjects: | CYAC: Fairy tales--Fiction. | Characters in literature--Fiction.
    | Princesses--Fiction. | Schools--Fiction. | Human-animal
    relationships--Fiction. | Fairy godmothers--Fiction.
Classification: LCC PZ7.C1364 Mis 2018 | DDC [E]--dc23 LC
record available at https://lccn.loc.gov/2018010618

Source of Production: Versa Press, East Peoria, Illinois, United States
Date of Production: July 2019
Run Number: 5015573

Printed and bound in the United States of America.
VP 10 9 8 7 6 5 4 3 2 1

For Michael, always

ONCE THERE WAS A GIRL...

Hold still. I just want to help you." I keep my voice calm yet firm. If she moves too quickly, she could do more damage. I need to be careful not to spook her.

"That's a good girl," I coo, taking a step closer. "Stay right where you are. You're safe now."

Crack! My bare foot snaps a twig, startling her. She hobbles farther into the brush, making it hard for me to see anything but her panicked eyes. If she moves any deeper into the branches, I won't be able to reach her.

"It's okay," I tell her as some of our friends quietly gather around to watch me work.

I step deeper into the thicket, the chittering of the insects intensifying in the shady trees that surround me. The air is hot, and I'm sweating despite having left my jacket and skirt back in the clearing. I snag a vine from above me and use it to tie back my pale-blond locks. She's watching with interest as I fix my hair.

"I'm not going to hurt you," I promise, my voice barely more than a whisper. Slowly, I pull something from my pocket I know she'll like. I place the handful of cashews I swiped from last night's dinner on a branch between us. She eyes the nuts for a moment, then quickly eats one. Nice!

As she crunches on the nuts, I stay very still, listening for any sounds. I hear an owl hoot in the distance and water babbling in a nearby brook, but for the most part, the forest is unusually quiet.

"Good snack, right?" I ask, trying to make her feel at ease. "I know I look young, but I have a lot of experience doing what I'm doing, so don't be nervous."

She tilts her head at me.

"It's true! Just last week, Nox came to see me for a sore throat, and I mixed him a tonic that cleared it right up. And when Peter lost his sense of smell after having a bad cold, I made a broth that fixed everything." I inch closer to the tangle of brambles where she's perched. She doesn't move, so

I keep talking. "And when Deirdre sprained her ankle after running from a bear in the Hollow Woods, I made her a splint, and now she's walking just fine."

I hold out my hand. She doesn't recoil, but she doesn't move any closer either. Time to bring out the big guns. I strain my neck toward my friends below me. "Deirdre? Can you please back me up here?"

Deirdre takes a flying leap, landing on the tree branch next to me.

Did I mention she's a flying squirrel?

Or that the "she" I'm trying to help is a songbird?

Lily, my bearded dragon, pokes her head out of my shirt pocket to listen to Deirdre's mix of clicks, clucks, and high-pitched squeaks that will hopefully get through to the little red bird with the injured wing. I can only make out parts of what she's saying.

I'm not fluent in squirrel yet.

Not like other humans! Really cares... Knows medicine! She can help... Trust her. We do! Friend!

I smile at that last word. I don't have many friends. When you tell the kids in the schoolyard you can talk to animals, most call you a liar. Or a freak. Some even say you're evil.

Hey, I get it. It's an unusual, uh, *talent* to have, but it's a big part of who I am. Besides, I am really good at this "helping animals" thing.

I notice her wing is sagging. She might have snagged it taking off from a tree, or maybe she bumped into a giant. My animal friends say it happens a lot. The songbird curiously sniffs my fingers with her beak.

"That's it now. Climb in," I say in a soft voice. Deirdre chimes in too, squeaking her encouragement.

Finally, after a moment of hesitation, the bird steps into my steady palm! Below, I hear the chattering cheer of my friends.

"What's your name?" I ask the little bird as I carefully cradle her fragile body.

She chirps in a small singsong voice.

"Scarlet? How lovely to meet you, Scarlet." I stand up and walk her over to my office.

My office is really just a quilt I stole from the maid's quarters. (Mother wanted it tossed anyway.) On the blanket, I have my satchel of herbs that I pinched from the kitchen and mending tools I've gathered from our sewing kits. I store everything in a hollow log near the clearing so no one questions what I'm up to when I go on my "daily walks" beyond our garden gates.

I rinse my hands with the little jug of water I've brought with me, then open my satchel and pull out the small fabric slings I've been making while Mother thought I was practicing my needlepoint. Finding one that looks to be the right size, I get to work, setting the bird's wing as best I can. Scarlet tweets excitedly when I'm finished. Then I mix basil, chamomile, and willow bark seeds together with the water.

"This should help with the pain," I tell her. "Come see me again in a few days, and we'll see how your wing is mending. If you want, we can help you find a safe place to sleep in the meantime." I place the mixture in a tiny thimble and encourage Scarlet to drink. After a few sips, she tweets at me excitedly, and I know she's saying "thank you." She has a sibling that lives in a hollowed-out old oak three trees over so she'll be safe there while she heals. That's a relief.

Everyone is so excited about Scarlet's new sling that they can't keep quiet. Between the neighs, snorts, and chittering from other animals, I'm worried a big, bad wolf—or worse, the main house—will wonder what's going on.

"Keep it down!" I say with a laugh. "You're going to give

us away!" The noise decreases slightly, and I lean back and soak in the sunlight filtering through the trees.

I live for moments like this. Being a creature caretaker is all I've wanted to be. Mother thought it was a phase I'd grow out of, which is why she didn't pay Father any mind when he bought me a leather satchel filled with "animal doctor" supplies. But ever since, I've been pulling spiders out of drinking jugs, mending birds' wings on my bedroom windowsill, rescuing wayward kittens from hungry foxes, and getting an occasional visit from a unicorn that has lost its sense of direction.

I won't be *growing out of it* anytime soon. I don't know how I'm able to talk to animals or know what they need, but I'm smart enough to know you don't give up a gift like that. I hope that someday even creatures beyond Cobblestone Creek will seek me out for help. But first, I need to find someone to teach me proper creature care techniques.

"*Devinaria!*"

I sit up straight. The birds stop chirping. Lily pokes her head out of my pocket again, and we stare at each other worriedly. No one should be looking for me out here. Not when I swore I was going to Mother Hubbard's Tea Shoppe with some girls from class.

"Devinaria! Where are you?"

Drooping dragons! The voice grows louder, and I hear trumpets sounding in the distance. It's as if a royal procession is about to roll right through the forest. I hear footsteps, then heavy breathing, as if someone's running in our direction.

I jump up, trying to put all my supplies away before someone sees them. Then I remember what I'm wearing. I look down at my undergarments and torn shirt and spin around in a desperate search for my skirt. The shirt and bloomers I'm wearing aren't much different from the outfits the boys in the village wear, but the ensemble is definitely not—as my mother would say—"princess appropriate."

"Princess Devinaria!" Our footman Jacques sounds out of breath as he stumbles into the clearing. "There you are!"

I cringe. I *hate* when people call me that. "Devin is just fine, Jacques." I try to maintain an air of dignity as I grab my skirt from a bush and quickly wrap it around my waist, pinning it on the side where I've cut it for easy on-and-off situations. With a ribbon tied and draped down the side, no one can tell I sliced the skirt open (other than Jacques, who has just seen my little trick and looks quite alarmed).

"How, um, did you even find me out here?" I run a hand through my hair and pull out a leaf. "Did you need something?" I ask him.

"Miss, it's urgent!" Jacques's eyes widen as the trumpets sound closer. "Your mother...father...the trumpets... Miss, *it's* coming, and..."

I inhale sharply and stumble backward. Lily flicks her tongue wildly. "No," I whisper.

"Yes!" Jacques insists, grabbing my hand. "Your invitation is here!"

ROYAL ACADEMY

From the desk of the Fairy Godmother

Headmistress Olivina would like to cordially welcome*

Devinaria Nile
of Cobblestone Creek, Enchantasia

to Royal Academy for her first year of princess training!

Please arrive with a training wand, mini magical scroll, several quills, and no fewer than three ball gowns, two petticoats, and three pairs of dress shoes. (Please note: Glass slippers should have scuffed soles to prevent injuries due to heavily waxed floors.)

Personal stylists and tailors will be on-site to assist all students in creating their signature royal style. We look forward to seeing you one week from today!

◇◇◇◇◇◇◇

The word welcome *is only a formality! Attendance at RA is* mandatory *for all young royals in the kingdom. Questions should be sent by magical scroll to the Fairy Godmother's office.*

CHAPTER 2

YOU ARE CORDIALLY INVITED

Jacques pulls me through the clearing, and I let him because I'm numb, numb, numb. I've been dreading this day for a long time. My heart pumps harder as we near the grounds of the cottage.

Okay, it's not really a cottage. I just call it that. It's a castle. The word *castle* just sounds so obnoxious. Like, "Sorry I'm late. It's a long coach ride from my castle." I hate when some of the kids at school say things like that. I hear the village kids talking about us sometimes. *Fancy-schmancies* they call our type. If only they could see what I'm wearing right now.

Mother is already pacing at the garden gate as we approach, and that's when I realize I have a bigger problem than the invitation to end all invitations. Such as the fact that my clothes are torn and I'm covered in dirt and leaves when I said I was going to Mother Hubbard's. I dig in my heels on the grass, and Jacques falters.

"Princess!" He strains to keep me moving. "We must… go… Wow, you're strong."

Hanging from tree branches all day is great for upper-body strength.

"I can't go, Jacques." I pull back. "I'm sorry."

"Your mother is waiting!"

"I can't let her see me like this!"

He pulls.

I yank his arm back. We could play tug-of-war all day.

"Devinaria?"

We both turn to the garden gate, where Mother is peering through the ivy that clings to the fence. She has an elaborate updo for a Tuesday afternoon and is even wearing her tiara. Seeing her makes my stomach start doing cartwheels.

I wave. "Hello, Mother."

She steps through the gate with a look of horror on her face. "You? You! *You!*" She's pointing and stuttering as she takes in my appearance. She touches my torn skirt and cries out. Jacques lets go of my arm and slowly steps away from me. He can sense a teakettle about to whistle when he sees one.

"You look lovely today, Mother! How was your luncheon with the royal court?" I curtsy clumsily.

"I left early when I heard what was happening. Get in the house this instant!" She grabs my arm and starts walking. "If we're lucky, we can clean your face and hands before they get here. They're already one château away!"

"How do you know they're coming here?" I ask as Mother pulls me through the garden gate where my lady-in-waiting, Anastasia, is…well…waiting. Her eyes widen as she takes in my disheveled appearance.

"The dove delivered the preliminary invitation to our doorstep an hour ago so you could be ready." Mother pulls a scroll out of her pocket and hands it to me. "And you're clearly *not* ready."

As I skim the scroll, I get a sinking feeling in my chest. "They need me there next week?" Now my voice is shrill. "That's not enough time! I…have nothing to wear." There's no greater travesty in Mother's life than not having the right gown, even for something as informal as a trip to the village.

She waves her hand around. "Of course you have things to wear! Darling, I've been packing your trunk for Royal Academy all year!"

I should have known. "But my hair and my nails... They're a mess!" I falter.

"Done and done!" Mother ticks off each concern with a joyous laugh. "I have maids inside now waiting to help. Devinaria, the *Enchantasia Insider* gives us hints on the week invites will go out, so I'm prepared." She pulls a twig out of my hair with a frown. "I'm sure they can do *something* with this bird's nest of yours."

My heart is pounding faster. It feels as though the garden walls are closing in. I pull away. "But I don't want to go to Royal Academy."

Mother's jaw begins to quiver. "That's nonsense! We've talked about this path for you since you were a toddler. This is your chance to move up the royal ladder! There hasn't been a widespread plague or dragon outbreak in years, so we both know being twelfth in line for the throne will get you nowhere. With any luck and perhaps some fairy magic, you'll meet a prince at Royal Academy so you can rule a small province or kingdom."

"Mother!" I sputter. I can see some of my forest friends peeking through the garden gate. "You'd want a whole village to be wiped out just so I could be queen?"

My voice is louder than I intended, and I realize all the servants are looking at us. Mother's face is crimson. She smiles brightly at them all, then turns back to me. "Don't be ridiculous, Devin. I was just pointing out how difficult your prospects are! What I'm trying to say is that going to RA will give you the best chance of becoming a queen."

"Who says I even want to be a queen?" I counter. "Maybe I'm meant to do something else with my life. Look at all the good work I've been able to do for the creatures of Cobblestone Creek." I motion to the fence. "I know you don't want to admit it, but I have a connection with animals. I can understand them and help them."

Mother turns me away from the servants. "Would you stop saying that?" she whispers. "You sound deranged! It's your destiny to become a ruler!"

"Ah, I see you found Devin." Father walks up behind us. He's dressed in his finest threads, a sash across his chest showcasing the many gold medals he's earned as a commander in Enchantasia's Royal Infantry. He kisses my cheek even though it's sweaty. "Ready for your invitation?" he asks me, but before I can answer, Mother cuts in again.

"Not exactly. She's still going on about her love of animals! We've put up with this childish hobby long enough."

Father puts a hand on her shoulder and says, "Belinda, you can't deny she has a gift."

"Gift? It's a *hobby*." Mother looks at the two of us as if we're conspiring against her. "You must stop encouraging her!" she says to Father, then turns to me. "This is not your future, Devinaria. Royal Academy is! Just look at your cousin, Penelope Claudine. She went to Royal Academy, and now she's married to a king with three castles!"

"I don't want three castles!" I protest. "I don't even need the one castle we have. It's too big."

"Oh, Devin, you're so charming." Mother takes my hand in her free one. She is smiling so earnestly that for a moment I feel bad about how hard I'm fighting her. "What is this really about? Are you nervous about going away to school? Because I am sure you're going to love it there. Royal Academy was created just a few years after your father and I were married, so I never got to go, but it sounds like a dream! Can you imagine having a royal tailor on hand to make you any ball gown you want?"

"But I don't want…" Never mind. I pull my hand away and fold my arms across my chest, ready to restate my case. I hear horses galloping in the distance. The trumpet sound is growing near. I don't have much time.

"Fight me all you like," Mother finally says. "Let your official royalty profile portrait be one of you looking like this! The truth is, you don't have a choice concerning whether you attend or not." She points to the fine print on the bottom of the scroll and makes sure Father sees it too. "All royals of your age must attend RA. It says so right here."

I bite my lip so hard I taste blood. The trumpets are growing louder. Suddenly, the servants open the back doors, and I see men wearing wigs and gold-trimmed white jackets. They're carrying my official proclamation as they march into our garden. There's also a painter with them who immediately begins to sketch my image.

"Her royal portrait!" Mother cries.

She wipes my face and tries to tame my hair, but my eyes are on Father. He's my one hope for avoiding a future that involves Royal Academy. "Father?" I say questioningly. "*Please.*"

I watch his expression closely. It wavers between sadness

and an emotion I can't identify. He places his hands on my shoulders as Mother tries to fluff my skirt. I watch her pull the ribbon out of her own hair and tie it around mine.

"Devin, I tried. I really did," Father says. "But she wouldn't budge on the matter. Even after I explained your extraordinary gift. If anything, it only made her want you more."

She? "You mean Mother?" I question.

Father shakes his head as more guards arrive. If they're surprised by my appearance, they don't say.

"Olivina," Father explains in a whisper. "Royal Academy's headmistress." His eyes search mine. "She says she can see the future, and you, my child, are destined for great things."

ROYAL ACADEMY

Student Supply List for Young Ladies

◇◇◇◇◇◇◇

If you don't have these books at home—and I expect many of you are well-versed in these teachings already!—please purchase and bring to the first day of orientation. I look forward to many fruitful discussions this school year.

—Headmistress Olivina

Reading List

¤ *Royal Academy Rules* by Fairy Godmother Olivina

¤ *Beyond the Glass Slipper: How to Nab a Prince without the Right Shoes* by Cinderella

¤ *Cursed Childhood: How to Avoid Being a Target for Sleeping Curses and Poison Apples* by Fairy Godmother Olivina, foreword by Princess Rose

¤ *Rescue Plans and Other Things a Princess Should Never Leave Her Castle Without* by Fairy Godmother Olivina

¤ *Ten Ways to a Happier Imprisonment* by Rapunzel

¤ *Mirror Image: Finding the Royal Within* by Snow White

Optional Reading

¤ *From Rags to Royals: 1,001 Beauty Tips from Princesses* compiled by Marta Marigold, RA's Official Beautification Expert

DON'T BE LATE
FOR AN IMPORTANT DATE!

Ever since my invitation arrived last week, it has been
chaos. Mother has been running around confirming
I have everything I need for school, and I've been making
checklists to ensure my animal friends are well taken care
of while I'm gone. I'm busy writing out my final creature
care instructions for Anastasia when a dove lands on my
windowsill. It has a scroll held tightly in its beak. The familiar
pink-tinted parchment tells me what I already know: it's yet
another decree from Royal Academy. So far I've gotten:

1. An invitation to First Knight Out, which is
   apparently a ball held on our first night there.
2. Information on how to book ball gown

fittings. "Appointments fill up fast!" the scroll blared in glowing red letters. (I crumpled that one up and used it as kindling for my fire.)

3. Details on new lady-in-waiting assignments. I'm appointed a "fully trained" one after arriving at RA and can't bring Anastasia. (She's been sniffling all week.)

4. Biographies on my new roommates. I haven't read those yet. (I cringe thinking of the one Mother must have written for me.)

What could RA have left to tell me? Do they need to know my glass slipper size?

"Greetings, Demetris," I say to the dove. "What's new?" I gently pry the scroll from the bird's beak, then slide over a small bowl of water I have ready for such visits. Demetris sips politely as I open the scroll. This one is a reading list from Olivina herself.

"Holy harpies! Why would I want to read *Beyond the Glass Slipper: How to Find a Prince without the Right Shoes?*"

"Oh, miss, I loved that book!" Anastasia pipes up.

Both Demetris and I look at her strangely.

"I know I'm not royal, but every girl should know the way to a prince's heart."

I stare at her blankly.

"Surely, you've read it, miss."

I shake my head.

"You mean, you've got your first ball tomorrow night, and you don't know how to act?" Her jaw drops as she moves toward me, retying the bow on my skirt. "Thankfully, I remember the book well. The most important thing to do is keep your eyes lowered the whole time so he can see your lashes. And only dance with him *twice*. The third time, run away and say you have a curfew or your coach is about to turn back into a pumpkin. That will keep him guessing."

What am I going to do with this girl?

"Anastasia, that sounds like terrible advice! Besides, I can think of plenty of reasons to run away from a boy that have nothing to do with dancing." I pull a worn book out of my drawer. "You should read something really helpful like *Red-y for Anything*. Have you read it?"

She shakes her head.

"It's the story of Red. You know, Little Red Riding Hood? It's about how she went from almost being eaten to becoming the fiercest warrior in the Hollow Woods. She's one of my idols. I'm sure this book is much more interesting than some boring book on balls and princes." I drop it into Anastasia's hands, and Demetris tweets his thanks before flying back to school. "Now let's go over those instructions I gave you one more time."

"I'm to go into the garden at least twice a week, maybe more if the weather is bad," Anastasia repeats. "I should replenish your supply of medicinal herbs and slings in the hollow tree near the large pine, and if the animals come pecking at your window while you're gone, I'm to tell them you're at school, then read to them from this scroll you've compiled of ailments and possible cures." Anastasia's eyes widen. "But, miss, what if they try talking to me? You know I don't understand them."

"It's okay," I tell her again. "I've already spoken to them, and they're just thankful you're going to try to help them while I'm gone." I glance at the packed wardrobe and trunk sitting near my door. "Which hopefully won't be long."

"But, miss…" Anastasia begins to say.

"Devin," I remind her. "We're the same age. You can call me Devin."

Anastasia lowers her eyes. "It doesn't feel right, miss. You're royalty."

When she makes comments like this, I want to hit her over the head with my shiny new training wand (which is not as fun as a mortar and pestle). "That's just a title. We're the same, you and me." I squeeze her hand. "I know I'm asking a lot, between taking care of the animals and sneaking around my parents, but I promise you, if I can find a way to get you into RA with me, I'll do it."

Her face crumples, and I'm afraid I've made her cry again. Instead, she curtsies. "That would be most wondrous, miss!"

We're back to *miss* again.

"Devin!" Mother's voice echoes through the palace. "They're coming! You should be waiting at the door!" I hear trumpets and know it's time.

Anastasia fixes the hairdo of braids atop my head, which I wanted instead of a normal updo. (Hey, all Mother said was that my hair had to be up.) But Mother won the battle over what I'm wearing. She says she heard Olivina puts a lot of emphasis on first impressions, so she has me in a baby-blue corseted gown. I'm not sure how I'm supposed to breathe or wave. (Mother says it's all about the carriage wave on the procession into school.) I'm changing out of this contraption as soon as I get to my new room. But before I head out on my journey, there is still one thing I have to do.

"Can you stall my mother for just a moment more?" I beg Anastasia.

Anastasia nods and hurries off, and I run to my window and look out. As I'd hoped, several of my animal friends have gathered in the garden. "Don't worry," I tell them, trying not to get choked up. (Anastasia's crying has thrown me off my game.) "I'll be home for holidays, and Anastasia is going to take good care of you till I find a way back myself." Deirdre glides from the tree to my windowsill.

"*Miss you! Olivina! Won't be back! Princess!*"

I'm still not fluent in squirrel so I only understand some of what she's saying, but I can sense her panic. "Don't worry. I'm not going to get distracted by all those princessy things at Royal Academy," I assure Deirdre. "I'll be back. You'll see!"

"*Devinaria!* They're almost at the door!"

"Goodbye!" I say as Deirdre keeps chittering. I give my bedroom one last look, then head downstairs. I stop short when I see what's going on. The castle's staff is lined up in our entranceway in front of the open door. Outside, villagers are gathered on our lawn, cheerfully clapping along to a band. Someone from *Happily Ever After Scrolls* is also here, reporting on the occasion. Drooping dragons! This is all for my send-off to school?

I hear a neigh and run down the steps to the doorway. My eyes widen. There are eight—*eight!*—horses attached to a ginormous pumpkin coach. A real pumpkin! I always thought Princess Ella was embellishing that vegetable transportation story, but here is an exact replica. I watch as a footman hoists my luggage onto the back, then turns and opens a door for me.

"Make way for the princess!"

I whip around. Gretchen, my neighbor, is holding a banner with my name on it:

Princess Devinaria of Enchantasia.
Long may she reign!

Reign? For Grimms' sake. I open my mouth to say something to Gretchen, but Father and Mother have appeared and each taken one of my arms to lead me to the coach. People begin to cheer, Anastasia waves a tearful goodbye, and the trumpets grow louder. I dig in my heels.

"Father?" I hesitate. I hate that I sound nervous.

"You're going to do fine," he assures me. "Just be yourself."

"But better!" Mother adds. "Be the princess we know you are."

Father gives my hand a squeeze and whispers in my ear. "I made sure to add a few of your favorite things to your trunk after your mother finished packing. Have fun." He winks as he hands me off to the footmen standing in front of the carriage. "You are special. Always remember that."

"And brush your hair a hundred times before bed each night," Mother adds. "It will really add luster to your locks." She touches the coach. "Now, don't forget to smile when you arrive. Everyone will be watching you—the *Enchantasia Insider* says pumpkin coaches are reserved for Olivina's most promising new students!"

I'm one of Olivina's most promising new students? The fairy godmother doesn't even know me. If she did, I'm pretty sure she would not consider me princess material.

Mother starts to cry, and Father hands her a handkerchief.

"Good luck, darling," Father says as the footmen help me inside. The cheering increases as we begin to move. "Write often! Send Pegasus Posts!"

"Always listen to Olivina!" Mother adds. "She knows best! After all, she's advised the most famous princesses in Enchantasia. And look how all their lives have turned out! Oh! And, Devin?" She runs after the coach. "Don't forget to call for a…before you reach school!"

"What?" I shout. I can't hear what Mother is saying, but it must not matter if she only remembered to tell me now.

The coach is already speeding me away from the only life I've ever known and barreling me toward a new one full of uncertainty.

IF THE PUMPKIN FITS

I've never been this far from home before.

We've been traveling for hours, but I haven't been able to stop staring out the pumpkin coach's window.

Mother has never liked to travel. ("When your home is this grand, why go anywhere else?" she always says.) Most of the ladies in the area come to our home for tea or to discuss local politics, so there's never a need to go anywhere but the village for dinners or to visit some of the shoppes.

But sometimes when Mother was busy and just Father and I were warming ourselves by a roaring fire, he'd tell me about some of the experiences he'd had with creatures during his adventures with the Royal Infantry—like facing banshees on the moors, outsmarting giants in the Highland Hills, and lulling dragons to sleep on a craggy cliff overlooking Tigers Eye Cove. Oh, how I wanted to make friends with a dragon!

"There's a whole world out there to explore, Devin, for men who are brave enough to do it," he'd say.

"And women," I'd add.

"And women," he'd add with a laugh. "Just don't get yourself eaten by an ogre."

I've never met an ogre. Or a giant. Or even a real fairy. With a small flutter of hope, I wonder whether I'll get to meet some new creatures at Royal Academy. All the famous royal stories have magical animals like dragons and griffins. Maybe Royal Academy won't actually be all bad.

My hands grasp the pumpkin door frame as we pass a small pond where two children are fishing. In the distance, the turrets of a castle loom. Suddenly, I hear shouting. A group of children are racing after the coach.

"Are you Princess Ella?" a boy shouts.

"Not even close!" I holler back, and one of the footmen looks at me.

Oh. I guess that response isn't very royal. I try one of those waves I always see the royals do when they pass through the village. The footman smiles appreciatively. *Score!*

"This is a pretty far drive," I say, hoping he'll forget what I said. "I didn't realize Royal Academy was this far from home."

"We had to go around the Hollow Woods, princess."

"Wouldn't it just be easier to fly on a magic carpet or something? Olivina's a fairy godmother. Can't she do all kinds of magic?"

"Yes, but it's tradition for new students to arrive by coach." The footman looks uncomfortable as he adjusts his cap. "And Olivina doesn't like RA magic used unless she's present. Too much can go wrong."

"You could take Pegasi," I suggest.

He looks even more perplexed. "Yes, but royals only use those for long-distance travel in emergency situations. Olivina prefers that royals travel in style. Hence, the pumpkin coach and white horses. Much more dignified. Are you comfortable, miss?"

"I'm fine," I insist, "but should we stop for a moment to give the horses a break? Or water?" I glance at the horses' backsides as they gallop along. "I'm sure they're tired."

"Can't, miss," he says. "We'd miss your entrance."

Entrance?

"And besides, we're close. It's just up ahead." He points at a dark line of trees on a knoll.

I don't see a castle. Maybe it's around the bend?

"Here we go, princess!" the footman tells me as the driver whips the horses. (Does he really have to do that?) We're headed for a giant redwood tree with no sign of stopping. "Hold on!"

"We're going to hit that—*treeeeeee*!" I scream as the horses race into the trunk. I close my eyes tight and brace for impact.

Huh? I open my eyes again and…holy harpies!

The trees shimmer and disappear like a mirage, hiding the real path to Royal Academy. It's no longer nightfall either. The sun is shining brightly as if we're on the other side of the world. Our coach slows down, rolling over a narrow bridge toward the largest castle I've ever seen. I stand up and lean out the window. The towering palace sits atop a rocky hill that reaches so high it looks as if it's in the clouds.

"Protection charms!" the footman yells to me. "Olivina is too smart to let the next generation of princes and princesses be seen before they're ready."

"Or kidnapped," adds the driver.

"Or put under a curse," adds the second footman.

I try not to think about any of those scenarios as I stare at the shimmering gray castle. It dwarfs what the royal court has going on. (Rapunzel, Rose, Cinderella, and Snow—Enchantasia's reigning princesses—all have castles that sit in a quad surrounding their headquarters.) This castle is ten times the size of that. It could be as big as our whole village! There's even a waterfall flowing from one turret. Hundreds of flags billow in the wind atop the turrets, the largest one spelling out ROYAL ACADEMY in gold, glittery letters. I blink fast. On the rocky wall that surrounds the hilltop compound, I see hundreds of small figures. We're still a distance away, but I can hear the cheering.

"Your family flag is above the main building, princess," says the footman, pointing toward a doorway that is two stories high. I spot the Nile family crest even from the distance. It has a painting of a river running through a Royal Infantry suit of arms. "It's rare for a first-year student to be flying so close to the school's banner, miss," he adds, staring at me. "Who are you related to?"

"Me? No one important." I point to myself. Maybe he hit his head on the bumpy ride. "I'm just Devin, remember? Devin Nile?"

He looks flustered. "No, I mean, if you're not related to someone important, why are you getting this much attention from Olivina?"

Before I can really ponder his question, the coach stops short. I look out the window and notice several bridges leading to the castle, all crowded with coaches waiting for their turn to enter. Mine is the only one that is a pumpkin coach.

"Are you ready, miss? This is everyone's favorite part!" the footman says excitedly.

"Ready for what?" I get the feeling I'm supposed to be doing something. I fumble around the orange velvet seat cushion in the hopes of finding some sort of "First Day" scroll, but there's nothing. My trunks are tied to the back of the coach, so any chance of consulting one of the books Olivina requested is out of the question. *Think, Devin!* What could I be expected to do right now?

The horses gallop faster toward a lowering drawbridge that connects us to the school grounds. The cheering grows as we ride up to an expansive courtyard and stop in front of large, sparkling double doors. I peek out and spy a velvet carpet that reaches from the coach all the way into the castle. It's lined with people wearing gray velvet dresses and suits. I hear a pop and look up. Fireworks are going off overhead. I do a double take as two blue songbirds fly into view carrying a banner between their beaks. It says WELCOME, NEW STUDENTS! *Holy harpies, this is intense.*

"Presenting Her Royal Highness, Princess Devinaria Nile of Cobblestone Creek," a crier shouts.

It's time to face the music, I guess. I take a deep breath and go to open the carriage door, but ropy vines are holding it tightly closed. "I can't seem to get out," I yell to the footman.

"Of course not, miss," he says. "We need your escort first. Is he here yet?" He looks around as one of the horses neighs. "Should we call for him?"

My shoulders tense. "Escort?"

The footman blinks, then pushes a white, powdered curl away from his face. "Your *prince* escort who will accompany you from the coach to the castle."

I hear what sounds like the impatient stamping of hooves and look back. There is a line of white coaches behind ours now. *Come on!* I hear a horse neigh. *What's the holdup?*

"I didn't know I needed an escort," I explain sheepishly as much to the footmen as to the horses. Some of the occupants are hanging their heads out of their coaches to see what's going on. "I don't have one."

My driver and the footmen look equally mortified—for me.

"Every princess who enters Royal Academy has an escort," the first footman says. "The girls who come are usually all over this stuff."

"I must have missed the memo," I say lightly. "Can one of you escort me then? I don't want to hold up the line."

They burst out laughing.

"A footman?" one of them asks incredulously. "Escort a princess? No, I'm sorry, miss. We can't. And you can't enter school alone either."

"Why not?" I ask, wringing my hands, which are starting to get clammy. I hear more neighing and wince.

"Because it's tradition."

Outside, the crowd starts whispering to one another. Lily climbs onto my shoulder, and I look at her. "Any chance you can turn into a princely escort real quick?" I ask. She blinks at me, then nods her head in the direction of my satchel. Curious, I open it and see my pocketknife utility tool glinting inside. My heart leaps. Father must have slipped it into my bag for me! I pick up the knife and eye the vines holding the carriage door closed. Waiting for an escort I know will never come has to be worse than whatever tradition I'd be ruining by walking into the castle alone. While my driver and one of the footmen confer, I start cutting through one of the vines. *One, two, three. There! It's loose.* I open the carriage door, and there is an audible gasp from the crowd as I hop out...solo.

"Miss!" The driver's eyes widen as I try to run past him. "You can't do that!"

"I'll explain my confusion, and I'm sure it will be fine," I say as Lily hisses at him, flicking a deep-red tongue in his direction. The footmen block my path. How rude! I fold my arms over my chest.

"Gentlemen, what seems to be the problem?" asks a boy who looks about twelve, just like me. At least, I think he's my age. His fancy jacket and gold sash make him seem older.

Finally! "Can you please tell them I can walk myself into school? It's really no trouble. I forgot to call for an escort, and they won't let me through."

The boy grins at me, then bows, giving me a great view of his head of thick, jet-black hair. "Hello, princess."

Everyone looks at me, including the boy.

Oh, they're waiting for me to curtsy, aren't they? I give a quick curtsy. "Hello." We look at each other. "Can I go now?"

He makes a face. "As much as I like a girl who can handle herself, I don't know if…"

"She can't, Prince Heathcliff!" blurts out my driver. "You know the rules better than anyone. She jumped out of the coach and tried to go inside *alone*. It can't be done, especially when she arrived by pumpkin coach."

He raises one eyebrow at me, his baby-blue eyes taking me in with interest. "Did she now?" He steps closer. "Have we met before?"

"I don't think so. My name is Devin," I say. And then I remember, with a sigh, that formality is the thing here. "Devinaria Nile of Cobblestone Creek so… Hey. Can you please tell them I can pass?"

He doesn't say anything for a moment. "Gentlemen, I'll escort her inside."

"That's really not necessary." I try again, an edge coming into my voice.

"Really, sir?" The footman ignores me. "Lady Clarissa Hartwith seems very keen on you escorting *her* inside." He looks over at a group of princesses who are hovering nearby, clearly trying to hear our conversation. The one in the middle looks angry. I'm starting to get angry too.

"Clarissa will have no trouble finding someone else," Prince Heathcliff says and flashes me a smile that makes his rosy lips stand out against his pale skin. "Shall we?" He offers me his arm.

I stare at it. "So you're really not going to let me go alone either?"

He looks momentarily baffled. "I can't do that, but as I said, I'm happy to help. And as all those staring princesses could tell you, I'm the best escort of the bunch today."

I wince. "Who are you?" I ask incredulously. "Prince Charming or something?"

He laughs. "Stop! How sweet. No, that name is already taken. My friends call me Heath." He holds out his elbow again.

That Clarissa girl and her friends are shooting daggers at me. I look away and try to ignore their whispers. ("Why did *she* get the pumpkin coach? I've never even heard of the Niles.")

My footmen sigh impatiently, and the horses are getting anxious. *Would you just go with him?* one says. *He's a looker!*

"Fine." I loop my hand through Heath's arm so we're interlocked. "But let's make this quick."

Heath looks offended. "Hey, I'm trying to help you. This is your first chance to be in the *Royal Academy Roster*."

"The *Roster*?"

He steps onto the red carpet, which begins to glow. The trumpets start playing again, and the fireworks resume. We begin the long walk up the red velvet steps to the sound of cheers.

He pats my arm. "Looks like someone else didn't read the books Olivina suggested. You really are my kind of girl. Thankfully, my twin talked my ear off about most of this stuff on the ride here, so I picked up a thing or two. You'll get the hang of it, I'm sure." The crowds begin to part for us, clearing the stairs.

"Who is *that*?" I hear someone say.

"It's Heathcliff! No clue who he's with," someone adds.

"I've never seen her before either. I thought he was escorting Clarissa."

I look back at Heath, who is smiling and waving to the crowd. "So is that Clarissa girl going to be really mad that you walked me into school instead of her?"

He shrugs. "Maybe. She'll get over it. It's only day one!"

He looks at me. "You were a smarter choice today. I can tell you don't want to make me your prince, which is a plus in my book. I have zero interest in finding a princess anytime soon." He winks despite himself. "Not when there are so many adventures to be had first." Talk about pompous.

"Presenting Princess Devinaria Katherine Nile and her escort, Prince Heathcliff Harold White the Third!"

The sound that comes next is so shrill that I almost let go of Heath's arm to cover my ears. It sounds like a hundred bats flying out of a cave at once, but it's not bats. It's girls. The princesses already inside the castle are screaming and holding up signs with Heath's name on them. One girl is jumping up and down and waving a sign that reads, SNOW GLAD YOU'RE HERE, HEATH! *Snow* glad? I do a double take at Heath.

His smirk returns. "Figured it out, huh? Snow White's younger brother, at your service."

Heath is *that* Heath? The one always being written about in *Happily Ever After Scrolls*? They love reporting on how he hangs out at Robin Hood's Archery Range in the village when he should be in school and takes magic carpets to exotic lands when he should be at royal court functions.

"Don't get weird on me now, Devilish Devin." Heath

winks at me again. I'm starting to wonder if he has an eye twitch. "We're going to be seeing a lot of each other. You're my sister Raina's roommate."

My jaw drops.

"I've seen your magical portrait for a week now, and I read your bio too, but it didn't do you justice. I had no clue you'd be this unpredictable." He grins again. "I like it. Now smile. We're about to make our entrance."

We begin to climb a never-ending staircase. Just when I think my feet are going to give out, we step onto the top step. I audibly gasp. The ballroom looks like it goes on forever and a day. Crystal furniture sparkles around every corner of the room, while wall-size tapestries portraying our reigning princesses hang above our heads. There is also a portrait I don't recognize. It's of a plump woman in an elegant silver gown and cape with curly blond hair and lots of jewelry. My eyes are drawn to the name glowing beneath her portrait: *Olivina.* I hear someone sneeze and look around. Seated to the right of us is the royal court, along with a figure whose face is hidden by a sparkling cloak.

The figure stands, removes her gold hood, and smiles beatifically. The royal court is all staring at her, and that's when I realize: It's the woman from the portrait! It's Olivina!

A hush falls over the room as Olivina eyes the two of us. Then she points a wand in our direction.

"Welcome to Royal Academy!" she says in a thick, throaty voice. And with a flick of her wrist, *poof*! We're gone.

PIXIES AND DRAGONS AND DRESSES, OH MY!

P *oof!*

Heathcliff is gone, and I'm alone in a long hallway where flickering torches cast an eerie glow. Curved stone arches and gargoyle statues tell me I haven't been sent home (*drat*) and am still somewhere inside the castle. My eyes are drawn toward several glowing signs on the walls. I step closer to read one and… *Zip!* A butterfly shoots past me. How did it get inside? I blink again and realize I'm not looking at a bug. It's actually a tiny human with wings, but it's not a fairy. Is that…a pixie? A flock of them suddenly flutter through the hallway, throwing confetti and singing.

Jumping giants, this is cool. I have to talk to one. "Hello!" I say to one flying past me.

Zip! It tosses confetti in my face and keeps going, its silver wings grazing my left shoulder. I can hear it laughing as it flies away. How hospitable.

"Excuse me, I don't know where I'm supposed to go, and I was wondering if you could help me."

Two pixies stop in front of my nose, look at each other, and giggle. One points to the darkened hall behind me. "Definitely that way," the boy one says in a high-pitched voice.

Skeptically, I peer into the darkness and see pixies zooming in the opposite direction. Wait a second. Pixies, pixies, pixies… what have I read about them before? *Think, Devin.* Don't they love to cause mischief? *Yes! That's right.* I can't take their advice. Maybe one of these signs on the wall has some better answers.

> *The Royal Way: There Is No*
> *Try, Only Triumph! —Olivina*

Not helpful, but maybe the next sign has something better.

> *When Life Gives You Poison Apples, Make*
> *Applesauce to Give to a Villain! —Olivina*

I'm not even sure what that means. I keep walking in hope of finding a clue to where I should be going, and a pixie flies into my forehead. We both scream.

"You could have killed me," the pixie shouts, her voice no more than a whisper.

"Sorry!" I rub my smarting forehead. "But I wouldn't have bumped into you if I knew where I was going." The pixie opens her mouth, but I cut her off. "Please don't say 'down the dark hall.' I know that's not true. Can you save us both the trouble and tell me where I'm supposed to be? I was *poof*ed here."

She crosses her arms and looks at me. "I don't have the time to show you," she snaps. "I'm very busy, and all princesses should already be in line."

"In line?" I ask hopefully. "What line?"

She slaps her hand across her mouth. "Wasn't supposed to tell you that," she mumbles. "It's down the *lit* hall. The one lined with other girls. Didn't you read Olivina's manual?"

"No," I admit sheepishly.

"You didn't read *Royal Academy Rules*? Just come this way. Not reading the manual, I swear," she says under her breath. But thanks to my super-keen sense of hearing, I hear her.

"I appreciate your help, Miss…?"

"Ava," she says and does a double take. "No one has ever asked my name."

"Really?" I say in surprise. "Well, how do people address you, then?"

Now she looks intrigued. "They usually don't. Let's go so I can get back to work. With the ball tomorrow tonight, there is much to do if I want to enjoy it myself."

"I forgot all about the ball." Ava almost flies into the wall in horror. As I turn the corner to follow her, I see a long line of girls in rainbow-colored gowns. There is a lot of squealing and chatter. "Thanks for your help!" I say. "One last thing: What is this line for?"

She flies backward and looks at me sharply. "To get your lady-in-waiting, of course. She'll take you to your room and coordinate all your appointments. You already have your tailoring sessions set up with Marta, right?"

"Marta?" That name does sound familiar.

Ava rolls her eyes. "Princesses these days. *Marta!* The royal tailor?" I try to look like I know what she's talking about, but she flutters to my nose and lands on it. "Did you take pixie dust to the eye or something? You should know all this. Day one at RA is the biggest day of your life."

I sigh. "That's what everyone keeps telling me."

She flies to my shoulder. "Look, don't beat yourself up, okay? Just get in line and your lady-in-waiting will explain the rest."

"Thanks, Ava."

Ava smiles ever so slightly. "You're welcome. Good luck!" She flutters away.

I join the line and stand quietly, listening in to snippets of conversations. ("Mother limited me to only *six* pairs of shoes in my trunk. Can you imagine?") I'm still half a dozen girls from the front when I hear something strange.

"*Psst.*"

I look around. None of these girls are trying to get my attention. They all seem to know one another, and a few are even giving me dirty looks. I suspect they're friends with Clarissa.

"*Psst!*"

There it is again. I look around and spot a hand waving wildly at me from underneath a table with a velvet tablecloth.

"Could you hold my place in line?" I ask a girl discussing glitter hair-care products with a friend. Both of them have their hair done up with glitter already—one in pink and one in purple—to match their gowns.

"Hold your place?" Pink Glitter repeats. "What could be more important than the line?"

The hand under the table is frantic now. "I...uh...need to use the little princesses' room."

"Can't it wait?" Purple Glitter narrows her eyes. "This line is no joking matter."

"I once held it twelve hours waiting for Prince Heath's carriage to come by in a royal procession," says Pink Glitter with a breathy sigh. "I didn't want to miss him."

"I can't hold your spot," Purple Glitter tells me. "Your placement is what determines your choice of lady-in-waiting. If you leave, I get a higher pick. Your loss." They both nod.

Pick? I'm sure I'll still get someone good. "Fine. I'll get back in at the end of the line." I step off and realize too late the line is now fifty girls deep behind us. Oh well. I make sure no one is looking at me, then crawl under the table to rescue the frantic hand waver.

When I do, I come face-to-face with a boy. He has brown skin and brown eyes, is wearing a gold vest with a ridiculously ruffled collar, and is shaking as if he's freezing.

"Hi," he says.

"Hi," I say back. "Um, I think you're in the wrong place. This is the girls' line."

"I don't want to get in the boys' line." His voice is panicked. "I didn't sign up for this."

"I know what you mean," I say. "All the pomp and circumstance and formalities. It's just the first day of school."

"I don't mind any of that." He eyes me suspiciously. "Who doesn't like fanfare? Or a ball where they're supposed to be serving coq au vin? It's my favorite dish to cook when I sneak into our kitchen. It's the dragons I'm worried about."

"Dragons?" I repeat excitedly.

"Yes, dragons!" His voice cracks. "A prince in line behind me said we have to fight one at the end of the first marking period." He runs a hand through his cropped hair. "Not a pretend dragon for class. A real one! I heard that and ran. I can't do it. I'm allergic."

He starts to hyperventilate, and I know what to do. I spot a crumpled bag that someone must have tossed, smooth it out, and hand it to him. "Breathe into this." This worked once with a squirrel who was having a panic attack over losing his lucky nut. I watch the boy breathe in and out slowly.

"Better?" I ask, and he nods. "So you're allergic to

dragons?" I'm skeptical. I've never heard of this condition before. "Are you sure?"

"Positive," he says defensively. "I've never actually *seen* a dragon, but I always sneeze when I'm near dragon's-tooth products."

I'm not sure that qualifies as a diagnosable dragon allergy, but I don't argue. "Just tell your professors about your allergies and I'm sure you'll be excused," I say. "But I wouldn't worry about meeting a dragon in general. They're actually quite friendly…if you lay off their nests."

"How do you know that?" he asks, sounding unsure.

"I haven't met a dragon yet, but I intend to. I've read a lot about them, and I know the fire breathing is just a scare tactic. They also hate eating charred dinner." He looks like he might pass out. "In other words, you'll be fine! You're not dinner or looking for an egg. If you run into one, try talking about the smell of pine. They love it."

"I'm not talking to a dragon!" He skirts away from me in horror. I think he might regret waving me over now. "I'm not climbing a tower either, or learning how to fence! I once got a splinter when I fell into our sword case at home."

"And you're sure you're a prince?" I ask skeptically.

He purses his lips. "Says the princess dirtying the hem of her dress by climbing under a table in front of all her classmates."

"Point taken." I sit down next to him and offer my hand. "Devin Nile."

He shakes it. "Prince Logan Nederlander of the Wetherby section of Enchantasia. It's rural. All we have are cows and sheep. You really want to meet a dragon?"

"Sure. My dream is to meet one with a toothache who lets me examine her," I say breathlessly. "I'm going to be a professional creature caretaker someday."

"But you're a princess," he points out.

"So? Why can't I be both?"

"Because that's not how it works," Logan says. "Look, I like the prince title myself. Carriage processions? Love them. Perfecting the royal wave?" His right hand moves slowly through the air. His technique is mesmerizing. "I excel. But I'd much rather be seated at a table with the royal court discussing how to make a cranberry apple soufflé than be out there slaying an actual dragon. I'm good with planning and measurements, but I'm not a fighter." He holds up his hands. "See how clammy my hands are? I'd slide right down a tower wall on a rescue mission."

"So what are you going to do?" I ask. "Do you think they'll let you leave and go learn how to be a professional chef?" I'm not sure how classes here work. And I'm starting to regret not reading that manual.

His face drops. "Never." We're both quiet. "For now, I guess I have to get back in line, mention my allergies, and meet my steward. You're right—maybe they will understand." He starts to smile again. "There's so much to do…between tailoring sessions, knighting ceremonies, and checking out the chef's kitchen. Maybe I can suggest some new recipes. Plus, if I'm lucky, I'll make it into the *Royal Academy Roster*."

"See?" I say. "You've found the upside already. Stop worrying about fire-breathers! Get out there and get some coke-ah-whatever you said before!"

Logan begins to crawl out from under the table, then stops. "Wait. How am I going to go back out there? It doesn't look good for a prince to be seen hiding under a table."

I nod. "Good point. I've already made a bad first impression on those girls, so why don't I take the fall for you? Maybe someday you can return the favor."

Logan grins. "Deal. You're not very princessy, but you're okay in my book, Devin Nile."

I wink and crawl out from under the table. The chattering stops, and girls look at me. "I dropped my pearl necklace. Has anyone seen it?" I shout, crawling around on the floor while Logan slides out from under the other side of the table and makes his getaway down the hall. "Oh look! An emerald. It must have fallen out of someone's crown."

"Mine! It's mine! No, it's mine!"

Princess after princess leaves the line and rushes to search the floor. It only takes a few minutes before the girls give up on finding the missing jewel and start arguing over who was standing where and whether a lost gem is a valid excuse for leaving their spot. By the time I make it to the front, there are only a few ladies-in-waiting left.

"Name?" asks a bored-looking elf sitting at a long white desk three times her size. A large stack of scrolls is piled on the table, while quills magically mark several other scrolls.

"Devin Nile," I tell the elf, and a quill magically writes it down. "Of Cobblestone Creek."

The elf points lazily to two nervous-looking girls my own age behind her. "You can pick one of them to be your lady-in-waiting. The princess from Raroway, whose carriage broke down west of the Hollow Woods and hasn't arrived yet, will get whomever you don't want."

"Oh!" I feel funny picking one while they're both standing in front of me. They're dressed in identical green gowns, white aprons, and small caps that cover their hair. But the girl on the right has modified her cap by adding a small brown ribbon wrapped like a rose that brings out her brown eyes. They look kind. She catches me staring and smiles sweetly. I smile back. "I'm not sure how to choose..." I hesitate.

The elf yawns. "Ask some questions from the manual."

That darn manual again. I'll just have to wing it.

"Hello. I'm Devin Nile." They both wave. "I was wondering if...if..." What do I need my lady-in-waiting to do anyway? The same things Anastasia does for me at home? Does that mean cover for me with Mother and help out with creature care? I can't really ask that with the no-nonsense elf listening. I rack my brain for a question, then think again of Logan. "Do either of you like...dragons?" Lily pokes her head out of my dress pocket to hear the answer.

The girl on the left shudders. "I hate animals. Such dirty creatures."

The girl with the ribbon lights up like a firefly. "I've always wanted to meet a dragon!"

Bingo!

"I'll take her, please." I point to Ribbon Girl, who squeals. (The other girl huffs and takes a seat on the ground to wait for the princess from Raroway.)

"Brynn Haun," she says, coming around the table and hugging me fiercely. She smells of oatmeal and coconut, which is a pleasant combination. "I'm so pleased to make your acquaintance, miss!" She brushes a stray dirty-blond hair from her face and pushes it under her cap. "I know you only had two choices, but I wanted you. I heard the others talking... You arrived by pumpkin! Very few princesses do, so I knew you'd be special."

Brynn grabs my hand before I can even say "It's nice to meet you too."

"Let's move!" she says, yanking me down the hall. "Your roommates are probably already taking all the closet space!"

ROOM TO GROW

rynn, could you please wait up?"

I'm huffing and puffing as I chase my new lady-in-waiting up the circular staircase. The tight space reminds me an awful lot of what I've heard about Rapunzel's old tower. I try to yank my large hoop skirt through another turn and get caught again. I hope each dorm room isn't housed in its own tower. I am *not* climbing stairs every day.

"Oh, Devin! I'm sorry!" Brynn comes running back down a few steps to reach me and pulls me and my dress through another tight turn. "I should have warned you about the ceremonial tower climb on the first day. You won't have to take these steps again, but as Princess Rule 5 in the manual clearly states: a princess should be ready to face any tower she meets."

For the love of Grimm, is that really in the manual? "I'm glad this is just a one-time thing," I huff. "I can't see Olivina doing this."

"Oh no, she'd never!" Brynn says with a laugh. "Fairy godmothers always travel by Poof Dust or bubble." I do a double take. "But I'm sure you knew that. It's in the manual."

"The stinking manual," I grumble under my breath. Lily pops out to give me a pointed glance. "Well, onward then. If it's the ceremonial princess way."

Brynn stays several steps ahead of me. We pass a mirror, and I catch a glimpse of my reflection. My tiara is hanging off, my braid has drooped, and my cheeks are flushed in an unflattering way.

"Hello!" says the mirror, and I jump as the glass seems to liquefy and turn blue, then purple. "You look lovely today! You're a princess who is always ready to dig in and help. I can tell! Always remember you shine! But"—his voice lowers—"fix your tiara. You wouldn't want anyone to call you a sloppy princess."

I quickly reposition my tiara. "Sorry…er, mirror."

"That's Milo the Magic Mirror," Brynn tells me. "Hello, Milo!" He doesn't answer her. Brynn drags me away. "He only talks to royals. He frequents hundreds of mirrors in the castle and tells the princes and princesses what they need to hear. And," she whispers, when Milo is far enough away, "he supposedly reports back to Olivina about you as well. Just a tip."

"Thanks for the tip, Brynn." I climb farther, past a pack of pixies going in the other direction ("You're going the wrong way!" they say with a giggle) and a group of self-sweeping mops. "You seem to know a lot about Royal Academy."

"I love reading the *Enchantasia Insider*," she confesses.

The *Enchantasia Insider* is a gossip scroll I've heard Mother mention. No one knows who writes it, but the author seems to know everything.

"I've studied up, miss, so I'm familiar with your course books, and I know the manual back to front. I can help you with anything you ask."

Thank the fairies! Especially since I don't even know where my manual is. I assume in my trunk. I clearly picked the right lady-in-waiting. "You must be the guide to have at RA."

Brynn stops short at the top of the stairs. I can hear squealing laughter and slamming doors coming from the hall ahead of us. A pixie flying by us shakes her head and mumbles to herself ("They all think they're the next Princess

Ella…") while ladies-in-waiting run trunks, blankets, and pillows to various rooms.

"Miss?" Brynn looks nervous. "If I'm being honest, you should also know I can't sew and I make a terrible cup of tea." She scrunches her face tight, and I fear she thinks she's about to be fired. "But I'm very loyal, a good listener, and I will try hard! Plus, the braids I weave don't unravel like the one you have right now."

I touch my hair self-consciously. "I'm not worried. Besides, I can make my own tea." She blinks in surprise. "And we have tailors, right? You don't need to sew for me."

"Okay," she says shyly. "I really thought no one was going to pick me and I was going to be sent home! My mother is sixty-fifth in line for the throne, so technically I'm a smidge royal, but since I don't have a title, Olivina won't let our family attend royal classes at RA."

Wow, she talks fast.

"Olivina doesn't want us getting any grand ideas about rising above our rank," she adds. "But at least I can be in the castle as a lady-in-waiting!"

I try not to look surprised. That seems like a strange thing for a fairy godmother to say, especially considering Princess

Ella used to be a commoner. "Well, if you want to study at RA, I can share my school scrolls. Maybe we'll both learn something."

"Really?" Brynn's face lights up. "I knew you and I were meant to be together! Olivina said I was destined to get a great princess, and she was right!" She grabs my hand and leads me down the hall past an elf crew delivering basins for evening washups. "Let's introduce you to your roommates. I'll be staying with their LIWs—ladies-in-waiting—in the room next door." We stop at room 215, and she points to the gold nameplate on the door. It already has my name on it. "Look!"

> *The Private Residency of Princesses*
> *Sasha Briarwood, Devinaria*
> *Nile, and Raina White*

"Well…" Brynn looks at me expectedly. "Do you know the secret phrase to open the door?" she whispers.

"Phrase?" I whisper back. "You mean there's no key?"

Brynn laughs. "You're so funny, miss! We can't use a key. A villain could get their hands on it and find you! To enter, you have to say your coded magic phrase. It's in your manual."

Grr...

"Thankfully, I've already memorized the phrase, and since I'm your LIW, I can also use it to enter," Brynn says. She places one hand on the door. "Starlight and fairies bright, let me enter my room tonight!"

The door begins to sparkle and glow. As it opens, we get a whiff of... *Cough! Cough! Cough!* What is that smell?

"Go on in," Brynn encourages. "I'll be next door if you need me."

"She's finally here!" A girl comes barreling toward the door and envelops me in a hug. I start to cough harder. "Marigold mixed with lavender and a hint of apple cinnamon!" she says, her voice bright and cheery. "It's our official room smell! Do you like it?"

We have an official smell? "Yes," I choke out. "But it's a bit strong."

"Like a princess should be," she says with a melodic laugh.

Her eyes are big and brown, and her skin is as white as, well, snow. A small crown is perched atop her hair with a diamond-encrusted *R* centered in the middle, and she's wearing the brightest pink dress I've ever seen. She looks like Heath in a dress, which means this must be Snow White's younger sister.

"I'm Raina White, your new roomie! Heath already told me all about you! We're twins." She hugs me again. "And that over there is Sasha Briarwood."

I look across the room and see Sasha at her desk writing furiously with a quill. She's wearing a sleek plum gown that makes her look years older, and her hair is a shiny pale yellow. Already tacked above her desk are snippets of scrolls, mini magical pictures, notes, and maps. Every few moments she looks up from writing and stares into a mirror she's hung above the desk. "Hey," Sasha says to the mirror.

I'm not sure if she's talking to me or the mirror. Is Milo here? "Hi," I say anyway.

"Can I tell her, Sasha? Can I?" Raina asks, ready to burst. She doesn't wait for an answer. "Sasha created *Enchantasia Insider*! The gossip scroll? Have you heard of it? It's this amazing service that tells you all the royal goings-on in the kingdom, but you can't tell a soul Sasha is the creator! It's roommate-privileged information."

"You write that?" I say in surprise. "But you're so…young."

"What's that got to do with anything?" Sasha asks, finally turning to look at me.

My cheeks begin to flush. She makes a valid point. I

hate when anyone tells me I shouldn't be a creature caretaker because of my age or my background. "I'm sorry. That was silly of me to say."

Sasha eyes me appraisingly. "I may only be twelve, but already I know more than two-thirds of the royals in this kingdom. I research all my stories and print the truth. Not the fluffy pretty stories *HEAS* wants you to believe or the proclamations the royal court sometimes puts out to calm their subjects' fears."

"Sounds sort of risky," I say.

"Which is why mum's the word," Sasha tells me. "I've decided to let you and Raina into my circle of trust, based on the roommate confidentiality rule. Don't make me question that decision," she warns. "I'm sure Olivina knows what I'm up to—she *is* a fairy godmother—but so far she hasn't cared. Probably because my rumblings are the real scoop on royal life and...oh." She looks into the mirror again and pulls at her right eyebrow. "It seems my eyebrows could use a plucking. Excuse me."

"Sasha is very into grooming," Raina says. "I know, I know, every princess should be! I am too, but Sasha is just so good at it." She sighs. "I guess that is what happens when your big sister is Princess Rose!" She laughs prettily. Everything about Raina is pretty.

At the name Rose, Sasha looks over again, her eyes narrowed and blazing. "Let's get this part over with. Yes, she's my sister, and yes, she's doing much better. She'll be back to public duty any day now. But more importantly, unlike my sister, I would *never* be swayed by a villain."

Wow, talk about intense. Although I guess I'd be pretty sensitive too, if my older sister had helped the evil witch Alva try to take over Fairy Tale Reform School. The room is so quiet that I can hear Brynn through the wall. "I've never met your sister," I say carefully, "but even if I had, I'm smart enough to know you are two different people."

Sasha surveys me closely. Her mouth curves upward slightly. "Good. I'm glad you get it." She goes back to writing.

"She's not usually so huffy," Raina whispers, pulling me away. "She's just got her tiara all bent out of shape because everyone here keeps talking about how she's Rose's sister and Rose went all villain for a spell. But Sasha is nothing like her. We've known each other for years. She's very focused on her scroll. We've been in our room three hours now, and she's spent two of them working and the other hour combing her hair. She says the scroll is her life's work and the whole reason she's here."

"My scroll is going to be way bigger than *HEAS* has ever been," Sasha declares as she plucks brow hairs. I didn't realize she was still listening.

Raina chuckles. "Oh, Sasha." She turns toward me and takes my arm. "Let's get you settled in, shall we? Your trunks already arrived, and they're massive!"

"Massive?" Sasha looks up. "Is it true you came by pumpkin coach? How did you get one? I've never heard of you or your parents, and there is nothing on you in my royal log, but you must be someone important." She walks across the room and stands so close that I can smell her rose-scented perfume. "So who are you really?"

"Devin Nile," I say evenly. "And I honestly have no clue how I got that pumpkin coach. I didn't even want to go to Royal Academy."

Raina gasps while Sasha raises her right eyebrow.

"Keep talking," Sasha says.

"I just mean, I already know what I want to do with my life," I tell them. "So why go to RA? I'm going to be a creature caretaker. I've been doing it for a while already. There's such a need in Enchantasia! We don't even have a magical care expert in the village back home."

"But you're a princess," Raina reminds me, sounding worried I've forgotten. "You have duties that are your birthright. You won't have time to do creature care once you're crowned."

"Raina, you don't really believe that, do you?" Sasha rolls her eyes. "Where does it say a princess can only do princess duties? I love a good pair of glass slippers as much as the next royal, but making this scroll a success is big for me too. I'd never choose one over the other. I want to have both."

I think I like this girl after all.

Raina frowns. "But Olivina says we all have a purpose, and we have to set an example for the kingdoms," Raina tells us. "We can't be seen acting *common*."

"My scroll is anything but common," Sasha says coolly and looks at me. "And being good with animals is not common either." The two of us smile at each other.

"I guess you're right," Raina says, scratching her chin. "I mean, my sister, Snow, has always been a friend to the animals, and they were a huge help when she was... You know..." Raina closes her eyes tight, and I think of Snow's curse.

Suddenly, our door opens and our LIWs are marching in, their arms stacked with pillows and satin blankets. "What will it be, my ladies?" asks an LIW. "Do you want one pillow, or are you planning to go all 'Princess and the Pea' and opt for a dozen?"

"Tickle me pink, it's a tough decision!" Raina says. "What do you think, roomies?" She lifts her skirt so it doesn't drag and runs to the LIWs.

And just like that, the mood lightens from talk of royal duties to something we can all get behind: comfortable bedding.

HAS ANYONE SEEN
MY GLASS SLIPPER?

After a dinner of roast duck and pheasant, I got a surprisingly good night's sleep on my official RA bedding (one pillow each for me and Sasha, "Princess and the Pea" treatment for Raina). The next morning, while Sasha works on her blog and Raina brushes her hair ("Ninety-seven, ninety-eight, ninety-nine… Today's goal is two hundred strokes!"), I decide to finally unpack my trunk. Guess it's time I accept I'm actually here.

When I unlock the trunk and open it, I recoil in surprise. Glitter headbands with bows? Three crinoline undergarments? A *pink* dress? *No, no, no!*

"Brynn!" I call out, wondering if she can hear me through the walls. "SOS!"

Our door opens within seconds, and Brynn rushes in. She looks from my alarmed expression to the trunk, closes the lid, and points to the label in confusion. It says DEVINARIA NILE on it in silver cursive.

"What's wrong, miss? Are you missing something?" she asks.

"No. I mean, yes… I mean, this can't be my trunk," I insist.

"But it is."

"It's really not." I show her the contents. "I've never even seen these dresses before!" I hold up a purple crushed velvet gown that must weigh ten pounds. "And my lady-in-waiting swore she packed my riding boots and my pants, but they're not here."

Raina looks up. "You own pants?"

"Jodhpurs," I say, feeling funny when I realize how put out my roommates look. "They're great for climbing."

"Climbing?" Raina looks even more alarmed. "Why would you want to climb something?"

"Plenty of reasons!" Sasha pipes up. "What if you need to sneak through a window, or climb into a carriage to eavesdrop on a conversation, or pop through a tunnel to get to a secret meeting spot?" Sasha ticks off her list as I nod in agreement. "But then again, I'd probably hire one of my writers to do that." She touches the satin on a green gown in my trunk. "I wouldn't want to ruin one of these glorious dresses." She holds it up for size. "If you're not claiming these gowns, I will."

"Ooh, I'll take some too!" Raina says.

The three of us rummage through the trunk. Forget the jodhpurs. More importantly, my animal kit is missing! And Lily's food! I mean, in a castle like this, I'm sure crickets are available, but I need my animal kit. What if I come across an animal in need? Father said he slipped some of my stuff in my trunk, but it looks like Mother got to it again before I left. I need to fix this. I put my fingers to my lips and whistle my patented distress birdcall.

"What are you doing?" Raina asks in alarm.

I ignore her and run to the window. No one comes at first. Then I spot a carrier pigeon hobbling along the windowsill, dragging one leg behind him. Hans Christian Andersen, he's hurt!

"Are you okay?" I ask, but the pigeon just blinks at me. Maybe he's in too much pain to speak, the poor thing. I look at the leg in question and notice some yarn wound tightly around it. It's cutting off the pigeon's circulation! Pigeons are always gathering string of any kind—straw, vines, yarn—to build nests, and sometimes they get caught in it. "Quick! Someone hand me their scissors." Raina runs over with a pair. "Don't worry, I can fix this," I tell the pigeon. Gently, I snip away at the yarn till I can get my finger underneath the tightest part of the string. The pigeon begins to move its claw as I remove the binds. When the string is off, he even takes a few steps. "There! It may still hurt for a bit, but you're free."

The pigeon coos. *Thank you! You don't look like the other girl, but when I heard your call, I came anyway. This message was for her.* He drops a scrap of paper in my outstretched hands.

I open it up. *T— She knows. Be careful. —B*

"What's that?" Sasha asks.

"I'm not sure." I put the note in my pocket to examine later. Another pigeon lands on our windowsill.

"What's with all the birds stopping by?" Raina asks as she tries on the purple shawl that goes with the dress I was holding earlier.

This is a pigeon I know. "Astrid, hi! Can you help this guy get to Anastasia to have his leg looked at? Then, can you please fly to my room, grab my animal-care kit from my bedchamber, and bring it back here? If I'm not in my room when you return, you can leave it on the sill, but it's important I get it right away."

Anything for you! Astrid tweets back. *My sister still talks about how you fixed her wing last month.* Then she flies off with my new little friend right behind her.

I turn around, smiling, then freeze when I see Raina's expression.

"That bird. It understood you. You can talk to animals? That's an upper, upper-level princess skill! In fact, I don't think any RA graduates have ever been able to do it, other than my sister, Snow, and well, Olivina."

"No wonder you got a pumpkin carriage!" Brynn says, clapping her hands excitedly.

"Where did you learn to do that?" Sasha asks, grabbing her quill.

"Wait!" I panic. "You can't write about this."

"Why not?" Sasha asks. "Do you realize how rare your skill is? You should tell everyone! You'll definitely land in the *Royal Academy Roster* for that."

"I don't want to be in any *Roster* or even rule," I say, exasperated. "Didn't you say there is some sort of roommate confidentiality agreement? For keeping each other's big secrets?" I say with a pointed look at Sasha. She rolls her eyes and puts down her quill.

Brynn nods. "Yes, it's in the manual."

"'Your roommates are your most trusted confidants, other than Olivina, with whom you can entrust your every wish, dream, and fear,'" Raina recites, her hand on her heart.

"And you can trust me, miss," Brynn adds. "I'm your lady-in-waiting."

"Thank you. This needs to stay between us," I tell the three of them. "People get funny when they know what I can do." I think of the kids at school.

"Really? I think it's incredible!" says Sasha. "Have you always been able to do this?"

I shrug. "Since I was little, I think. Not all animals, though. I'm not well versed in squirrel, and toucans have a dialect that I haven't mastered, but I can generally understand most creatures, which really helps with creature care. It's why I want to do it so badly. I feel like I'm meant to do this more than anything else in life."

"But Olivina won't allow you to be anything other than a ruler!" Raina blurts out, and Brynn looks at her scuffed shoes.

"Didn't you just say Olivina can talk to animals too?" I try. "Maybe she'll understand."

"Maybe," Sasha says, but she doesn't sound convinced. "I'm not sure she's known for being understanding."

Before I can ask what she means by that, the door to our room opens again, and Raina and Sasha's ladies-in-waiting come rushing in with fabrics, jewelry, and bags overflowing with shoes.

"It's the five-hour mark till First Knight Out!" Raina says, forgetting about our conversation. "Fairy be! We should have started getting ready ages ago."

I look back at my trunk and frown. "Brynn? Can you pick me out something to wear to this thing tonight?"

Everyone in the room stops what they're doing and looks at me.

"You mean you haven't decided what you're wearing yet?" Raina blubbers. "This dress is important! It's the first time you're being seen by the whole school! It must be one of a kind! Didn't you pick your tailoring up from the Royal Underground on your way to the room?"

"She doesn't know what that is," Brynn says quietly. "She didn't read the manual, and she has no tailoring appointments." My roommates gasp.

"Guilty as charged," I admit. "Fashion just doesn't really mesh with my creature care interests. But it's no big deal. You just said you liked the dresses my mother sent. I'll wear one of those."

Sasha's lady-in-waiting drops the silver bag in her hands. Pearls spill out of it.

"You can't wear one so ordinary!" Raina cries.

"Ordinary?" I question. "I thought you guys said these dresses were nice. It's just a dress, after all. I'm not trying to negotiate a peace treaty." I laugh to myself. The others don't join me.

"For Grimm's sake, Devin," Sasha groans. "You can be into creature care and still care about looking decent. There is nothing wrong with knowing the difference between taffeta and chiffon dresses. In fact, I'm going to make sure I teach you, but for now…" She looks at the others. "Ladies, we have a royal emergency on our hands. She can't wear dresses this ordinary."

The group of ladies-in-waiting and roommates gather together. There is a lot of whispering, then mumbling. Fabric goes flying, and Raina yells, "She'll win 'Most Likely to Be Taken in an Ogre Attack' if you have her wear *that*!"

I know better than to open my mouth. Finally, they turn

to me. Why do they all look like someone just said the castle's been cursed?

Raina pats my hand. "Now, we don't want you to worry. Everything is going to be fine!"

"There's no way we'll get you an appointment with Marta now," Sasha adds. "But we have enough original gowns to go around this evening so we'll share."

"Then tomorrow, first thing, Brynn will make you an appointment in the Royal Underground so this never, *ever* happens again," Raina adds. "Okay?"

Does this require an answer? "Okay."

Brynn waves me over to a chair where she has set up an assortment of beauty equipment I've never used before. Sasha is throwing dresses her way, and Raina struggles under the weight of a large wooden jewelry box.

"Great!" Raina says. "Let's make you princess perfect for your First Knight Out."

"If not princess perfect, then at least princess passable," Sasha says dryly.

But I never get a chance to respond because *eep!* Brynn is already plucking my eyebrows, and it hurts!

Fairy be, what have I gotten myself into?

Royal Academy Rules

PAGE 17

BY FAIRY GODMOTHER OLIVINA, FOUNDER
AND HEADMISTRESS OF ROYAL ACADEMY

An All-Important Guide
to RA Superlatives

On Sunday evenings, before the start of each new school week, the *Royal Academy Roster* scroll will arrive under your dorm room doors. The anticipation is always palpable! The results are sometimes unpredictable! Superlatives are won by popular student vote. While there is a standard list, students are also allowed to create new titles to write in, making this a popular activity! The *Roster* has become a fun tradition at Royal Academy that helps princes and princesses put their best sword or glass slipper forward.

These superlatives are not fluff! Nor are they meant to discourage you! Public perception is a crucial tool for any ruler. Loving subjects are loyal subjects! The Royal Academy staff will be watching the weekly results closely. While these superlatives are not grades, per se, they are a guide to tell us how well you're doing—or not doing—among your peers. We encourage you to read the superlatives and let them inspire you to improve your status each week. Prove to us whether you are better suited to lead an army or clean the palace dishes.

So what will you win your first week here?

Most Likely to Forget It's Midnight, or Princess Most Likely to Snag a Prince by the End of Year One? The results, dear students, are up to you!

Love, Olivina

DID SOMEONE SAY
THEY WERE HAVING A BALL?

S top pushing!"

"I'm not pushing!"

"My family is eighth in line for Elderberry's throne. Yours is fourteenth. Obviously, I should be ahead of you."

"Hey, watch my tiara!" a girl says as her crown is nearly knocked off.

"Ooh, I love your tiara. Where did you get it?" asks the other girl.

The long line of princesses waiting to enter the First Knight Out stops arguing long enough to burst into giddy laughter—the light, airy, princess kind my mother has tried to teach me for years. I'm too itchy to try it. This plum-colored dress Sasha and Raina insisted I wear is impossible to move in and so *hot*. There must be ten layers of lace, satin, and beading. It looks like a wedding cake. "Ten minutes, and you'll forget you even have it on!" Raina swore.

I haven't come close to forgetting. I look around for a distraction and notice the paintings on the walls. We're in the Hallway of Honors, where the portraits of princes and princesses who came before hang for all to see. From Cinderella to Hua Mulan to Prince Sebastian, a.k.a. the Beast, the royals have one thing in common—they're all painted at their coronation ceremonies with Olivina standing next to them.

"I don't know how she manages to be there for every royal," Raina says admiringly when she catches me staring. "We are so lucky to have her at RA. Everyone thought she'd retire by now, but the fairy godmother never seems to age!"

"Good genes," agrees Sasha. "We need to find out what she uses for face cream." She snaps her fingers, and a quill flies out of a fold in her dress, along with a scroll of parchment. She writes the question down. "Actually, beauty secrets of fairy godmothers would make a good post."

"My sister never would have found her happily-ever-after without Olivina," Raina adds, staring at her sister's portrait.

"How so? She would have said no to the poison apple?" I ask somewhat jokingly.

"No, silly!" says Raina. "Olivina was the one who suggested my brother-in-law, Prince Adam, try to rescue her with true love's kiss." She sighs. "It's so romantic."

Sasha snorts. "An eternal coma is not romantic. Neither is being locked away in a tower waiting for a prince to rescue you."

"It's all part of the process! You know that. All I know is I'm ready for my moment, whatever it is, and it starts with getting onto this week's superlative list." Raina poufs the sleeve of my candy confection of a dress. "We may even win the roommate award. We make a stunning threesome."

"That we do." Sasha admires her updo in a mirror. "It took an hour to get my hair up under this tiara."

"Beauty can be a pain!" Milo chimes in. "But it's well worth it when it creates a true vision like yourself."

"Thanks, Milo." Sasha blows him an air-kiss.

"Ladies! May I have your attention?"

I notice a well-dressed elf in a gray satin gown, half our height but standing on a box. She doesn't look happy. "Ladies?" she tries again, but her pip-squeak voice is drowned out by all the talking. Finally, she snaps her fingers, and a bullhorn appears in her hand. "*Ladies!*"

Everyone jumps. "Thank you for your attention! I am Fairy Godmother Olivina's EPA, Hazel Crooksen. In a few moments, you will be ushered through these doors and presented to the teaching staff as well as to your potential future princes. I expect you all to—"

"Excuse me?" A princess with blue hair waves frantically. "What is an EPA?"

Hazel's mouth tightens. "Elf personal assistant. Now as I was saying…"

"If you're Olivina's elf personal assistant, why aren't you in the manual?" The girl pulls a well-worn copy of the pink book out of a hidden pocket in her gown.

Hazel smiles thinly. "You wouldn't find me in your manual. I work for Olivina, not the students at RA, so my inclusion or omission from that manual has no bearing on the instructions I'm about to give. May I continue?" The girl nods, her cheeks reddening. "As I was saying, you should present your best princess self to Olivina and your teachers. This is your First Knight Out, meaning it is also your opportunity to make a great first impression. So straighten those tiaras!" Everyone around me touches their head. "Chins up!" We lift our faces. "Skirts poufed!" The sound of crinoline swishing takes over the hallway. "And we are walking, walking, walking. Stop!" Hazel listens at the door. "Okay, the boys are done, and now it's your turn. Smile!"

"We should hold hands and present a united front," Raina says as she watches the girls ahead of us proceed through the gold doors in a slow, two-by-two fashion. She frowns. "Hey! Why is Amber Arnold of Longtome going third? I'm higher ranked than her."

I glance at Sasha. "She probably got here earlier because she didn't have a twenty-minute shoe debate that made her roommates almost tardy," I say as we start to move forward.

"It was a tough decision! Beige and off-white are two different colors," Sasha points out.

Raina is now clutching her chest, her face full of panic. "What if some worthy prince sees Amber before me and is smitten? What if my future rule comes down to this moment, and I've already blown it?" She begins to hyperventilate.

I fan her with the wide sleeve of my dress. "It's going to be fine."

"Chin up! Smile!" Hazel admonishes us as we walk into… *Holy harpies.*

Now I see why my roommates were so worked up about shoes and line placement. First Knight Out is clearly a big deal. The ballroom of Royal Academy might be the most magnificent sight I've ever seen. The enormous room is lit entirely by clouds of glowing fireflies that float near the ceiling. Flowers crawl down the walls like ivy, while dozens of beautiful potted trees give the room the illusion of an enchanted forest. Just in case anyone forgot where they are, the RA insignia is stamped everywhere. Banquet tables line the walls, giving way to a large dance floor where a pied piper is playing the flute. Behind him, an entire band of musicians dressed in their best is serenading us as we walk in. Beyond the band, I can see the princes lining the walkway. They bow as we pass. Heathcliff winks at me, but Logan is too nervous to even make eye contact. He keeps dabbing his sweaty brow with a handkerchief. At least he made it to the ball. I give him a quick wave.

Then it's time for our last entrance step. Before we take our place along the edge of the dance floor, we curtsy to Snow, who is seated center stage and talking to a tall, reedy man in a deep-red velvet suit. To his left sit an elf, two fairies, and Princess Ella.

"There's my sister," Sasha says, sounding slightly annoyed. Rose is blowing kisses and throwing, um, roses, to excited students. "Guess she wouldn't miss her first chance to party."

"Where is Olivina?" I thought she'd be watching everyone make their first entrance.

The band begins to play a waltz, and Raina frowns. "I don't know. I thought we'd be announced before we were expected to find a boy and dance and…oh!" A young prince with bright-red hair holds out his hand to Raina. She giggles politely and nods.

"Well, that's one down and…oh." I turn around and realize Sasha has been whisked away by a dark-skinned boy with the greenest eyes I've ever seen. I can't even catch her eye as he twirls her away like a professional. "That leaves me."

It's okay. I'm not overly concerned with finding a dance partner. Instead, I move to the side of the room to watch the matchups and spy Logan sampling finger food. I start to make my way over to him, but stop when I see him walk away from the table and approach a princess I recognize. *Oh fairy be, no. Clarissa? Don't do it, Logan!*

Clarissa is wearing a gray gown with a skirt covered entirely in what seem to be peacock feathers, making her look like a rainbow. My eyes narrow. Those feathers better be fake.

"May I have this dance?" I hear Logan say.

Clarissa stops talking and looks at him, her lips curving into a slight frown. "Do I know you?"

"Not yet," Logan says shyly. "But one turn around the dance floor, and you won't forget the name Logan Neder—"

"I'll pass," Clarissa says flatly, and I hear a few girls giggle. I watch her attention turn toward Heath, who is standing against a wall looking at himself in a small mirror. Clarissa looks from Logan again to Heath, then frowns harder. Logan's face plummets.

Oh no, she didn't! I move swiftly to his side and grab his hand. "Are you Logan Nederlander?" I ask. "*The* Logan from Wetherby who has four castles…one for each season?"

"Er…yes?" he says unsurely.

"Oh good! I was hoping to find you before someone snatched you up. Any chance you'd ask me to dance?" I try to do one of those airy giggles I hear the other girls doing. The girls are all watching us with wide eyes, and even Heath looks up, so I must have nailed it.

"With pleasure!" Logan takes my hand, and within

seconds, he's twirling me so swiftly that the bottom of my dress flutters out like a parasol. He spins me left and right, clearing the dance floor as people stop to watch us, including Heath and a blond who has just draped herself on his shoulder. His mouth gapes. So does mine.

"I didn't expect you to know how to dance," I say.

Logan smiles mischievously. "I said I didn't like dragons or physical activity. I didn't say I couldn't dance. Mother made me take lessons for the past five years." He dips me. "I've gotten quite good."

"I'll say."

Logan pulls me back up, then spins me out again. "Thanks for saving me back there."

I roll my eyes. "She's not worth your time."

"I see that now," Logan says midtwirl.

"How's your roommate situation?" I ask as the room whirls by me.

We hold hands and spin around the perimeter of the floor. "I'm rooming with this guy Pierce Anderson. Comes from Hallockville. He brought a knife sharpener for his swords and has lifting equipment stored under his bed." Logan gives me a hard look. "I have a feeling we're going to be best mates."

I laugh. "Well, I'm with the sisters of the royal court." He raises his right eyebrow. "One is deeply offended by all my fashion choices, and the other is obsessed with being the perfect—" We hear laughter and turn around.

Raina twirls past us with her red-haired beau. "Oh, Linus, you are charming! What a delightful story about your castle's goat farmer!"

"Princess," I finish as Raina spins away in a cloud of apple fragrance, which I remember is her family's signature scent. "They're not so bad though," I say with a small smile.

The music suddenly stops, and everyone turns to the banquet table where Princess Ella is ready to address the crowd. "Students, it is my honor and privilege to welcome you to the school the royal court and I called home for so long."

"Wait, she went here?" I hear someone whisper.

"Yeah, after she ditched the Wicked Stepmother and won the prince," someone replies.

"Many of you think you know our stories," continues Ella, "the ones involving poison apples, glass slippers, and ivory towers, but there is so much more to those tales than what you've been told, and much of that involves the ways Olivina and Royal Academy transformed our lives. Before I met my fairy godmother, I was a lonely girl in rags, but after…" She smiles. "Olivina helped me see the real me. Princesses aren't princesses because they wear a crown. Princesses are princesses because they want to be leaders, game changers, and make a difference. I hope your time here helps you to grow in the same ways I did. Who will you be when you leave this school in four years? The answer is up to you"—she pauses—"and Olivina, of course."

The professors all laugh.

"That's for sure," Logan mumbles, and I look at him. He looks around to make sure no one can hear us. "My brother, Archer, told me Olivina and the staff set you up so you wind up living the life they want you to live."

"What do you mean?" I ask as Ella starts telling a story about how Olivina came up with the glass slipper idea.

"Archer had played knight since he was two," Logan tells me. "We all thought he would lead a dragon rebellion someday, but then he came to RA and the knight talk disappeared. Suddenly, he wanted to spelunk for jewels and explore uncharted territories." He makes a face. "He'd come home for family gatherings, and it would be all 'Olivina thinks I should…and Olivina says I'm meant to…'" His eyes widen.

"What if Olivina wants me to be a dragon slayer even though I want to—*Achoo!*—cook or run royal court meetings?"

"She wouldn't make you do something you didn't want to do," I say, but I feel suddenly unsure. "Maybe she just helped your brother see what he was really good at."

"He hates confined spaces," Logan points out. "Why would he choose a career that put him in caves?"

Before I can answer, Princess Ella makes her introduction. "So without further ado, I present our esteemed headmistress and legendary fairy godmother...Headmistress Olivina!" Ella motions to the ballroom doors. Two hundred bodies turn with her. The doors don't open. "Presenting Olivina!" Princess Ella tries again. I notice Princess Snow and the man in the red velvet whispering with Ella. Suddenly, the doors burst open.

EPA Hazel Crooksen comes running in wearing one shoe and a slashed-up skirt. "We've been breached!" she screams. "A flock of harpies has captured Headmistress Olivina, and they're heading this way! Run!"

HOLY HARPIES!

id Hazel say *harpies*?

I don't have to wait long for an answer. Seconds later, a flock of dark-gray creatures flies through the ballroom doors. A harpy snatches Hazel with its talons and flies off with her as princesses shriek in panic. Guests start stampeding in all directions, including the dance floor where Logan and I are standing.

I know I should run, but I stand there wordlessly staring at the creatures flying above us. I've never seen a harpy before. They look different from their drawings in my books. For one thing, their skin is more wrinkled and weathered, and their black hair is stringy and matted to their warty faces. One spots me looking and comes swooping down in our direction.

Logan yanks my arm, does a knee drop, and pulls me

under a punch bowl table before I can even blink. "Harpies?" he shrieks, starting to sneeze as the sound of screaming grows louder. "Wow, am I allergic to harpies too?" A rogue glass slipper rolls under the table toward us.

"We're sitting ducks! We can't stay under here." I lift the tablecloth and watch the pandemonium. "We have to help them!" I look to Logan. He's already crammed into a corner and is shaking.

"I can't!" he says. "I don't even have a magic wand or a training sword yet. How did they get into the school? RA is supposed to be the safest place in Enchantasia! That's why I wasn't nervous about going here. Other than the potential dragon fights. But…harpies? I-I… *Achoo!*"

"Help me!" I hear a familiar voice scream. I look under the tablecloth again and see Raina being carried off by a harpy. The two of us lock eyes. "Devin, get help!" she cries out.

"One has my roommate," I say, feeling desperate. "We have to help her."

"Harpies can't be stopped!" Logan says. "You should know that. Haven't you read about them in all your creature care books? We should just try to find a way to escape ourselves and then get help."

My creature care books! Logan is right. I must have read something about harpies. *Think, Devin. Harpies...* Oh, I know! "They can't be killed," I remember suddenly, "because they're undead."

Logan looks like he's going to pass out. "That's, uh...not very helpful."

I try to remember more over the sound of all the shrieking. "They're usually found on stormy and windy nights, they love trinkets and shiny things, and they hate music."

"But there isn't a cloud in the sky tonight." He points to one of the windows.

He's right. That's weird. I know I don't remember much, but I have to do something to help Raina. Maybe I can rationalize with them. "I can't just sit here, and I'm not going to flee." My heart starts to pound. "I'm going in. Wish me luck," I say, and without hesitating, I slide out from under the table into the mayhem before Logan can stop me.

There's lots of running, screaming, and shrieking, but I try to focus. The first thing I notice is the professors are missing— whether they've been taken or ushered to safety, I'm not sure. There's no sign of Hazel or Olivina either, but along one wall, I see several princes have overturned banquet tables. They've turned it into a miniature bunker and are now attempting to throw things at the harpies. They haven't hit one yet. A few princes are even charging at the flying beasts with their swords. One of them is Heath. He spies me out in the open at the same time I see him and comes rushing toward me.

"Come with me!" he shouts. "We have a guarded area where all the princesses are staying till this is over." He points to a corner of the room where princesses are huddled under tables while princes stand guard. As we're watching, a harpy flies down, picks up one of the princes, and carries him off.

"Safely guarded, huh? I'll take my chances on my own," I say.

Heath looks at me like I just said I have a giant for a first cousin. "Don't be stubborn… Ahh!" A harpy swoops down and grabs Heath's sword out of his hands. "That was an accident… No!" A second harpy reaches down and plucks him from right in front of me.

"Heath!" I go charging after the harpy.

What do I? What do I do?

"Give it your jewelry!" someone shouts. I turn around and spot Logan sticking his head out from under the table.

My jewelry… That's it! They love shiny things! I rip off Sasha's glittery silver bracelet and beckon the harpy closer. Then I pull off Raina's pearl necklace and hold both in the air. "Here harpy, harpy, harpy!" I call out. The beast turns around, Heath's ruffled dress shirt and jacket held tightly in its claws. "Want some jewelry?" It flaps its gigantic wings my way. "Want it?" I edge closer.

"Devin, stay back! I've got this," Heath says as he struggles to break free.

I wave the pearl necklace higher. "It's a nice, sparkly necklace," I say. "And so is this bracelet. So which do you want? Shiny jewelry or smelly prince?"

The harpy drops Heath to the floor and grabs the jewelry. Heath looks up at me in surprise.

"You're welcome," I say and hold out my hand to help him up.

Health takes my hand. "I had it covered."

The harpy flies off, squawking as it rejoins the rest of the beasts, which seem to be regrouping and heading toward the gathered princesses, including Raina. The princes are still trying to fend them off, but they won't be able to much longer.

"Stay away from them!" I shout without thinking, and a

few harpies look our way. *Oops.* Heath and I start backing up. I should have made a plan first.

"What do we do?" I ask Heath.

"*Now* you ask me that? I don't know!" he says, looking around for a weapon.

"Devin, sing!" I hear Logan yell. At the sound of his voice, a harpy turns toward Logan. He quickly drops the banquet tablecloth again.

Sing! "That's right! They hate music," I tell Heath. "If we sing, it might be enough to drive them to retreat."

"They closed the doors to the ballroom," Heath points out. "If I can get them open, you can lead them out with song. Distract them for a minute while I try!" He winks at me as he runs off. "I can't wait to hear your voice."

Oh bother.

I open my mouth and start to sing off-key. "There was an old lady who lived in a shoe…"

A window shatters overhead, showering the trapped students with glass. The screams get louder, which only makes the harpies go wilder. No one can hear my voice now.

I spot Heath pulling the first door open and hear more shrieking. The harpies are headed his way!

I'm running out of time. Looking around for something, anything that could help, I notice the band equipment lying on the floor and smile. Mother always did want me to learn how to play the violin. I race for the instrument and feel around under a broken cello for a bow. Quickly, I pull it over the violin, making the most ear-piercing sound I've ever heard. (And I've been present at a falcon baby hatching.)

As I'd hoped, the harpies stop what they're doing and look around for the culprit. I run the bow over the strings again, stretching the sound out even longer, and the harpies begin to claw at their ears. Heath noisily gets the second door open, and the harpies race toward him.

"*Sing* again!" Logan's voice rings out from his hiding spot.

A better song… I need a better song. Oh, I know!

I open my mouth and belt out a song Anastasia always sang as she drew my bath: "Listen, Enchantasia, to the song that's in my heart," I sing as I follow the harpies to the doors to make them leave. "It's an ode to you, steadfast and true. We'll never be apart again. Even when I'm leagues away, across the land and sea, I feel you with me, every day. For home, you are, to me."

Screech! The harpies are leaving!

My warbly voice might not land me a spot in the Royal

Academy a capella group, but it's repelling the harpies. They keep backing up to the exit, covering their ears with their talons. Thank goodness Heath is clear of the doors now. I rush toward the exit, still singing, to push the stragglers out. Our plan is working!

"Listen, Enchantasia, to the song that's in my heart…" I sing, but I'm not watching where I'm going, and I wind up tripping over one of the layers of my ridiculous skirt. Within seconds, I'm sprawled across the floor, the wind knocked out of me. Which means I'm no longer singing. Which means a harpy is headed my way.

"Devin, sing again!" Heath and Logan cry, but I don't have to. Strangely, the harpy doesn't lunge for me. Instead, it spins faster and faster, till the room is buffeted by an indoor windstorm. I shield my eyes from the flying debris. I feel someone grab my hand. It's Heath. We huddle together till the wind dies down. When I open my eyes again, I gasp.

In the place of the harpy is Olivina, dressed in a dazzling gold-embroidered gown. She reaches out her hand, and in a daze, I take it.

"Hello, Devinaria Nile," she says. "I've been waiting to meet you for a very long time."

I'm Your Fairy Godmother

Y ou've been waiting to meet me?" I ask, feeling disoriented.

"Yes!" Olivina says with a blinding smile as students come out of hiding. The teachers appear from behind a wall that reveals a hidden room, and Hazel arrives, looking no worse for wear. (Her dress is repaired, I notice.) "Let's give our new students a warm round of applause for their valiant efforts. What a wonderful job some of you did on your first test!"

Everyone starts to applaud as if they know what she's talking about.

"I don't understand," I start to say. "The harpies were part of a test? Couldn't they have hurt us?"

Olivina and Hazel glance quickly at each other. "There

will be time for questions later," Olivina says pointedly. "Hazel, get Miss Devin on my calendar."

Someone clears their throat. Heath is still standing behind us.

"Hello, Headmistress. You look lovely this evening. Even after transforming from a harpy!" He straightens his jacket. "I just wanted to mention I had a hand in this save-the-school exercise too. You know, in case you're already grading us for our superlatives or giving students days off."

I roll my eyes.

"You did magnificently, Heathcliff! You acted exactly the way the manual instructs for situations such as this," Olivina says. "If it had been a real harpy attack, princesses waiting for a prince to valiantly save them would be the right approach." Her eyes move to Logan. "But I can see there is still much room for improvement from our princes. It's my job to keep you all safe, and keep you safe I will, as long as you follow the rules of…"

"The manual!" the entire room shouts.

She turns to me, her golden dress gleaming in the ballroom light. "Miss Devin, your bravery today is commendable!" I smile. "You showed such strength, as I suspected you might, even if you did not follow protocol." She gives me a look, and Hazel tsks.

Protocol? Some of the princesses are whispering and shaking their heads at me as if I royally messed up. But how? I was only trying to help. I thought the school was under attack. I'm about to say that when I see the hard stare Sasha is giving me from across the room. For some reason, I get the feeling Olivina won't like my answer. I open my mouth, then close it when I see Sasha giving me a hard stare that seems to say *can it.*

"I'm sorry," I say instead. "I didn't know it was a test. I was just trying to help save as many students as I could."

"Of course, child! Your efforts were very valiant!" Princess Ella walks over, smiling. "We couldn't be prouder of a new student!" She puts her hand on the headmistress's shoulder. "And, Olivina, we're just glad you're okay. We didn't know you were testing the students."

"Darling, it wouldn't be a test if word got out, would it?" Olivina says impatiently, and they laugh.

Olivina waves her wand, and the room returns to its pre-harpy-attack state.

"Headmistress?" I can't help myself. I have so many

questions! "About the harpies. I'm so confused. Were they real? Were we in any danger?"

Olivina frowns. "Forget my schedule. Let's talk now, shall we?"

She waves her wand again and—*Poof!*—I am no longer in the ballroom. Instead, I'm standing in a beautiful green room with velvet curtains, couches, and tablecloths. The furniture is made of glass, as are the walls, which give floor-to-ceiling views of the darkened school grounds. One wall in the room is solid and covered with mirrors and framed photos of Olivina with famous royals. One of the mirrors is showing a direct feed of the ballroom. Everyone is dancing again as if nothing ever happened.

"Would you like something to drink?" says Olivina, waltzing into the room with a smile as if *poof*ing her students to different locations is something she does all the time. She goes to the glass table and picks up an empty pitcher. "Black cherry elixir, perhaps?"

"That's my favorite drink!" I marvel.

"I know!" Olivina says with a laugh. "Why do you think I suggested it?" She tips the empty pitcher toward a glass, and it fills with the dark red concoction. "Have a seat. You seemed so worried down there that I thought a little chat was in order right away. The last thing I want is for you to fret. And besides, I think it's important we get to know each other better."

I take the glass. "Thank you," I say as I sit down. Olivina taps the table, and food instantly appears. But not just any food. She's magicked in all my favorites—gooseberry pudding, patty cakes, cherry cobbler, and roast turkey. I'm half weirded out and half excited at the idea of a delicious meal. That harpy fight took a lot out of me. "You seem to know a lot about me already."

Olivina places a napkin on my lap. "I know everything there is to know about you, Devin. Your name appeared on my list for Royal Academy the day you were born! That doesn't always happen, you know. Many students' names appear when they are a year or two away from joining us, but you…" Her blue eyes are clear as water. "You have always been special. Clever! Bright! But I'm sure you knew that. It's not every princess who can understand animals."

I nearly drop my glass. "You know about that?"

She nods as she cuts us each a piece of pie. "Yes, darling! I've been watching the work you've done with the woodland creatures near your garden gates for years. Some have even come and told me tales of your kindness." She smiles. "I've been very impressed with what you've accomplished on your own, with no tutelage."

"Thank you!" I gush and take the pie. "I was hoping I'd get to talk to you about this. I'm sure there are other princesses who would love to do creature care like I do. Maybe if RA began to offer more classes for students with varied interests, it would help each of us find the right path. I feel like I already know mine, but there is so much I still have to learn."

Olivina puts her cup down. "All princesses' paths are the same. To rule our kingdoms. To set an example for the commoners around us. And to do what is best for their people, putting their needs before their own." She touches my hand. "I appreciate your gift, and I think together, you and I can cultivate it so that it best serves your needs as a royal."

"Needs?" I'm confused.

Olivina nods. "Yes. Needs. If we had the animal world on our side when it came to villainy, think of what good we could do! It's a wonderful gift, Devin, but it should be used as a tool to help you *rule*. It's not meant to be your true calling."

I feel my stomach tighten.

"You're meant to be a great leader! And I can help you

become one! It's my job to help show you the way. That's why you arrived by pumpkin. It's why I knew of you so early. Your ascension has been foretold, and it's my job to help you stay the course." Her tone changes. "But as you know, fairy tales can turn quickly. If you don't learn to harness your gifts and follow the rules, your happily-ever-after could disappear in a blip." The food on the table, including the pie on my plate, disappears.

"I wasn't trying to disobey." I feel the hair on my arms begin to stand up. "I was just trying to save my roommates."

"I know that, dear." Olivina tuts. "But that wasn't your role to play, was it? You were supposed to let the princes do that. If they can't rescue, what are they good for?"

"But I was the only one who knew how to handle the harpies." I don't understand what I did wrong. "I thought if I didn't do anything, someone would get hurt."

Olivina frowns. "You're overthinking things! Everything was fine. They were all under my control."

"But harpies are really dangerous," I remind her. "We didn't know you were controlling them." I hesitate. "This seems like an extreme test for our first week of school."

"That's not your decision to make," she snaps, and I stop

talking. Olivina quickly pats my arm. "I don't mean to be cross! I just mean, fairy godmothers watch over you, but they can't prevent bad things from happening. Our best defense is to show you how to help yourself—using the royal manual I've carefully and painstakingly put together based on past events. That is why I orchestrated this evening's challenge. To teach you how to react when faced with danger. You can understand that, can't you?"

Olivina is staring at me so intently that I say, "Umm, sure?"

She smiles. "That's a good girl! You know, I have a lot of experience taking care of royals like yourself. I've been doing it ever since I helped the royal court with their fairy-tale endings years ago. After Fairy Tale Reform School opened, I had a vision of a school of my own where I could guide royals the way I did Snow, Ella, Rapunzel, and Rose." She laughs.

"Oh, I know! Such lofty goals for a lowly fairy godmother. That's what I was back when Ella was a scullery maid and working for her wicked stepmother. But when I heard her cry for help, I knew I had to do something. So I sent her to the ball. I gave her the tools she needed to make the prince realize she was the one for him. It worked, and I helped elevate a commoner to princess status! But I couldn't stop the Wicked

Stepmother from treating Ella the way she was treated." She squeezes my hand. "Ella had to overcome that." Her face clouds over.

"That's what has always troubled me as a fairy godmother. I can grant wishes, but I can't stop villains from trying to destroy them." She looks at me clearly. "Enchantasia can be a dangerous place for a royal. There's a constant target on your back. Villains are always plotting...even right now... to destroy you and your kind. You know what they've done to the princesses of the royal court. What they want to do to your generation is even worse!"

I try not to look as alarmed as I feel, but somehow Olivina senses it anyway.

"Don't worry, darling. We won't let villains' dark deeds snuff out your royal future," she says. "Not under my watch. If you're all taken away, who will fulfill your duties and lead Enchantasia?" She leans forward so that our noses are practically touching. "*That's* why my tests are so hard, Devin. It's why I'm willing to use harpy attacks to make my point. My job is to make you strong enough to withstand the evil in this world. With me at your side, and my expertise at your fingertips, you can do that and so much more."

"I think I understand," I say slowly. At least, I'm trying to. My empty plate fills up with sweets again. "And I want to be ready to fight whatever evil comes my way, but..." I hesitate. "Wouldn't I be just as helpful to Enchantasia if I used my strengths to care for its animals?"

Olivina puts an arm around me. "You're a smart girl, Devin. I don't often meet with first years, but I could tell this whole experience has been a bit overwhelming for you. You grew up with a father who let you roam the forest and a mother who tried hard to teach you the ways of royalty. Those conflicting thought patterns would confuse any princess! I'm here to help you. That's what fairy godmothers do!" She scratches her chin. "I tell you what... If you want to continue creature care while working on your princess studies, I can make your wishes come true."

"Really?" I perk up. "That would be wonderful! Thank you!"

"It's fine for you to have some fun while you're at RA, but remember, things are done a certain way here. We have rules for a reason, Devin." She wags her finger at me. "And if you break those rules, there will be consequences." Her smile fades. "Flunking out of here doesn't just strip you of your crown; it strips you of Enchantasia."

I feel like the wind has been knocked out of me for the second time tonight. "You mean I'll be banished if I don't follow the rules here?"

She smiles again. "No need to worry. That's not going to happen to you. Let's consider tonight's catastrophe as strike one! You'll rebound. I'm sure of it!"

"Strike one?" I repeat.

"Well, I can't let you slide, can I? I have to show you've learned a lesson. Following the royal rules keeps us all safe," she says pointedly. "Remember what I've told you tonight, and we won't have any future problems."

I suddenly feel cold, and I have an overwhelming desire to flee, but I don't want Olivina to know how anxious I am. I attempt to smile again.

She opens her arms wide. "Now let's hug and have you on your way back to the ball. Look how much fun they're having!" She points to the mirror showing the ball's live feed. A second mirror is watching the professors' banquet table. Can Olivina see what's happening in our rooms too? My stomach flips at the thought, but I dare not ask her.

So instead, I hug her back and say exactly what she wants to hear. "Thank you, Olivina. For everything."

Olivina pats my shoulder. "That's what a good fairy god-mother is for."

She waves her wand over my head and… *Poof!* I'm gone.

CHAPTER

11

WHITE AS SNOW

oof! I'm back in the ballroom, standing in the middle of couples laughing and swaying to the music. I quickly move to the side of the dance floor and try to breathe slowly.

Did the fairy godmother just threaten to banish me?

I need air.

Spying an open doorway to the courtyard, I rush outside, past princes and princesses lingering in the doorway. "Where's her escort?" I hear a princess whisper, but I don't care.

This is the first time I've breathed fresh air since I arrived at Royal Academy. I look up. The sky is almost fully dark, except at the furthermost edges where deep purples and reds linger. Lanterns light the path, allowing me to make out small signs that say MAGICAL PUMPKIN PATCH, FAIRY GARDENS, and WISHING WELLS. I walk along and breathe more freely as the sounds of the party dim. Then I spy a sign that puts me completely at ease: STABLES.

Stables. Animals. My home away from home.

I run down the path, stumbling in my heels and voluminous skirt, neither of which are meant for speed. Boy, do I miss wearing pants.

I reach down and pull off my heels, walking barefoot. When I spy the barn, I break into a run again, throwing the doors open and soaking up the warmth of the room. It smells like a mix of corn and so much hay that I sneeze.

"Bless you!"

I jump. "Who said that?"

Princess Snow appears around a corner, a comb in her hand and a red blanket draped over her arm. Her scarlet dress is covered in hay dust. "Hello there! I didn't mean to startle you. You're Devin, right? My sister Raina's roommate?"

"Yes." Am I supposed to curtsy in front of the royal court? Or am I not supposed to curtsy since we're both royal? Oh, why didn't I read that darn manual? "I'm sorry to intrude. I didn't know anyone was in here."

"You're not intruding!" Snow rubs the nose of a white horse that has stuck his head out of his stall. "I'm happy for the company. I just came out to make sure the horses weren't spooked by the harpies." She raises her right eyebrow. "What's your excuse for being in the stables during your first ball?"

My cheeks feel warm. "With the harpy attack and getting called to Olivina's chambers…I was feeling a bit overwhelmed." I pet the mane of a nearby gray horse. "Being with animals relaxes me. When I saw the sign for the stables, I came running."

The horse neighs softly. *Harpies. Here, at Royal Academy. Can you believe it?*

I grab a brush from the counter in the stall and brush his back. I'm not sure I want Snow to know I can understand creatures yet so I talk generally. "I'm glad everyone is okay and the harpies are gone."

"Me too." Snow keeps brushing. "But some of these steeds are still worked up. They can hear harpies from a mile away, so they've been a bit agitated. I thought some warm blankets and a bit of brushing would do them good. Want to help me?" she asks. "It shouldn't take long with the two of us."

"I'd love to." I smile, and we get to work.

In what feels like no time, we've gotten the horses brushed and covered, and the incessant neighing that filled the air when I arrived has decreased. By the time we put everything away, I think I actually hear a few horses snoring.

"Thank you," Princess Snow says as we up lock the barn. "You obviously know horses. Do you ride?"

I shake my head. "No, but I've spent time around wild horses. All kinds of creatures actually. It's kind of my thing."

"Mine too," Snow says. "I'm working on instituting a creature care class this year. I'd really like to teach the students how to commune with our forest friends."

"Really?" I look up, excited. "I was just telling Olivina how badly I wanted a class like that." I'm talking fast now.

"Well, maybe it will happen, then!" Snow says. "She's supposed to give me a decision tomorrow. It's taken me a while to convince her we need a class like this, but I think she's finally ready to come around. The relationship between a royal and a trusted animal is one that can be very beneficial to both sides. What Olivina wants for all of us, more than anything, is to feel safe and secure in our roles."

"Does she?" I ask before I remember who I'm talking to. "I don't mean to be rude. I just came from Olivina's study." I hesitate. "I got in trouble for how I handled myself tonight."

Snow smirks. "I'm not surprised. Olivina is very old school when it comes to traditions and her teaching methods, so you leading the rescue was a bit much for her, but personally I thought what you did was very valiant."

"Really?" I ask hopefully.

"Yes, but it's not the way here," Snow says, and my face drops. "Olivina doesn't mean any harm; she's just a worrier. She's seen what happens to those who let villains distract them. It's not that she doesn't want a princess to take care of herself. She just wants to make sure you remember what's most important...being a good leader. Do you understand?"

"I guess." I'm still not sure I'm convinced, but I won't tell Snow that. "I thought she was just into parties."

Snow laughs. "She loves those too! All the glamour of being royal appeals to her, but the purpose of RA is for her to mentor royals. She does it well. Olivina helped us through our hardships, and when we overcame those things, we were that much stronger. Why do you think we have a Dwarf Police Squad now? I'm the one who made sure we started protecting the village. Ella worked with her formerly wicked stepmother to start a school for students on the path to wickedness. And look at the fine students Fairy Tale Reform School is churning out. Olivina helped us get there." Snow takes my hand.

"She wants to do the same thing for you. If she was upset, I'm sure it was just that your mess-up reminded her of another student who caused some problems in the past." Her face is momentarily troubled. "You seem like a girl who is going places, and I think a princess like you, Devin Nile, will find a way to rule exactly the way you've always planned."

I feel myself blush. "Thank you."

"Shall we head back to the ball?" she asks.

"Yes!" I say without hesitating.

Because when Princess Snow tells you exactly what you need to hear, you can't help but be excited about your future.

ROYAL ACADEMY ROSTER

Your first superlatives are here! First Knight Out edition!

- **Best updo:** Sasha Briarwood
- **Best dancer:** Logan Nederlander
- **Most likely to rescue a princess from an unexpected attack:** Devinaria Nile
- **Most likely to sweep a princess off her feet:** Heathcliff White
- **Most likely to be rescued by a prince:** Amber Arnold
- **Best dressed:** Clarissa Hartwith
- **Most likely to be eaten by harpies:** Emerson Bloomswood
- **Cutest shoes:** Cameron Highland

- **Best dressed roommates:** Clarissa Hartwith, Jillian Hyacinth, and Ramona Mills
- **Most likely to turn into a hag:** Natasha Eavesdone

<><><><><><>

Milo the Magic Mirror's weekly tip: Pinning up your hair requires more than three pins. Keep that updo tight so it can survive a waltz or a giant attack!

Want to know if you Reign or you're Ruined? Check back every Sunday for new superlatives!

ROYALS UNDERGROUND

R ise and shine! It's a new day! Put your best princess foot forward, and choose stylish but sensible flats as you'll be doing a lot of walking."

I jump up from a sound sleep to Milo's voice. *Pop! Pop! Pop!* Suddenly confetti rains down on the room, fluttering around and getting stuck in my surprised, open mouth.

"What is happening?" sputters Raina. Her hair is in curlers, and her sleep mask is still covering her eyes. "Why is it raining indoors? Who cast a spell in here?"

"We're up! We're up!" Sasha sputters as two pixies hang a FIRST DAY OF CLASS banner across our bay window. "Are we going to be woken up this way every morning?"

"Yes!" the pixies shout happily, still throwing confetti in my direction.

A loud gong drowns out our talking. Milo's mirror light dims, and a new voice sounds from the magical loudspeaker system.

"Happy first day of class, students!" Hazel says. "You'll find your class schedules with your ladies-in-waiting or stewards, along with plenty of time scheduled in between classes for primping or training." Sasha raises her eye mask and looks at me.

A pixie drops a pink envelope onto Sasha and Raina's beds at the same time Ava chucks mine at me. *Grouch!*

Raina squeals. "Look! It's another ball invitation!"

"Already?" I peel my envelope open. "We just had one last night."

"They're weekly or biweekly here," Sasha tells me, reading her own invite. "But this isn't a ball. It's a save-the-date for the Fifteenth Anniversary Spectacular of Royal Academy." She grabs a quill and starts taking notes. "Wow! It's just a few weeks away. We really need to order gowns."

"Don't forget to get those wardrobes finished!" Hazel says as if she can hear Sasha. "Wardrobe inspections will occur by the end of the week. A fine wardrobe could land you in the superlatives. Speaking of which, your first edition of the *Roster* was delivered overnight. One change to note: write-in superlatives by students are no longer allowed. See you around the castle!"

I can hear the screams throughout the floor. Raina springs toward our dorm room door and snatches the glittering scroll. Her eyes flash back and forth as she skims its contents, and I watch her face drain of color.

"But"—she flips the scroll over to see the back—"I'm not on here!" She looks at Sasha and me accusingly. "Only you two are!"

"Me?" I question. "That's impossible. I…" Got in trouble. Even got a strike one. Do my roommates know? "What did I get?"

"'Most likely to rescue a princess from an unexpected attack,' which was definitely a write-in superlative," Raina says accusingly. "And Sasha got best updo."

"Well, that's no surprise." Sasha touches her curlers. "My hair didn't move at all last night. It's this new hair-shellac potion I concocted, and it—"

"Clarissa won best dressed *and* best roommates!" Raina

interrupts. "How can that be? My gown was imported and took six months to hand bead! And a boy won cutest shoes. What is happening here?" Raina lets the scroll of superlatives float to the floor and stumbles back to bed. "I don't understand. I looked picture-perfect. I reacted the way a princess *should* when under attack—accepted it with grace and waited for my prince to come. And yet, I didn't get a single mention! Snow got in the *Roster* every week she was here. Heath is in this week's too, and I'm not. This is dreadful. I've failed my family." She pulls her blanket over her head.

I look at Sasha for help, but she's already at her vanity taking out her curlers. I pick up the list of superlatives and read them again. The students picked me? But what I did goes against everything Olivina says we should do during an attack. No wonder she's getting rid of write-in votes! No matter. I'll just have to really wow her this week with my princess knowledge and aptitude. Just as soon as I find my manual.

"It's only the first scroll," I say soothingly as Lily pops out of my nightshirt pocket and nabs a passing fly. "I'm sure you'll do something really impressive and get on there this week."

"That's easy for you to say," the blanket tells me. "You already had a private meeting with Olivina. I bet it was glorious."

I hesitate. Part of me wants to talk to someone about how strange last night was, but Sasha and Raina's families are super close with the fairy godmother. I bet they'd think I was just overreacting about her comments. "It was good, and I'll tell you all about it sometime, but right now I need your help, so get dressed."

"You need my help?" The blanket shifts slightly.

"Yes. Didn't you say I needed to go to the Royal Underground and have dresses made?"

My roommates scream so loudly that Brynn comes running into our room.

"Devin finally realizes she needs new clothes!" Raina tells Brynn. The two jump up and down excitedly.

"But wait," Brynn says, fixing the cap on her head. "Devin doesn't have an appointment yet. I've tried calling the Underground six times since we opened Devin's trunk, and I can't get her in till November."

"November?" I cry.

"Well, the anniversary invite just came out, and all the ladies-in-waiting rushed to make appointments." Brynn looks at Sasha and Raina. "You both have yours next week."

"Thank God." Raina clutches her chest. "We have to

get Devin something sooner." She goes to our magic mirror and taps it lightly with her training wand. "Milo, darling, could you be a dear and get me Marta, please? I'm sure she's already up working."

"Raina, *darling*," Milo says. "Students can't use their mirrors to summon others. Only Olivina can do that."

"Well, Olivina would want my roommate to look her best for classes, and I know my sister, Snow, would be upset to hear you couldn't make a simple connection for me when asked," Raina says, and I watch her in wonder. "Especially when you've been looking for a way to get a mirror in Snow's private chambers for months. I could put in a good word."

Milo's mirror begins to swirl red. "Patching you through. You owe me." Raina smiles triumphantly.

Suddenly, I see a room filled with gowns and multicolored fabrics. A short, broad woman wearing a sash of pins pokes her head into the frame.

"Raina! How lovely to see you, sweet pea!" Marta says. "I thought your appointment was next Monday. I just confirmed." She puts her hands on her hips and purses bright-orange lips. "You're not canceling, are you?"

"Of course not, Marta, sweetums, but I need a huge

favor! I know Snow and I would be ever so grateful—and would consider having you do *all* the gowns for our family's upcoming reunion ball—if you could squeeze in a teensy, tiny appointment this a.m. for me."

"For you, dear?"

"No, actually, it's for my roommate, Devin Nile. She can't get an appointment till November."

Marta's smile fades. "That's what happens when you don't reach out to your seamstress first thing when you arrive! I assumed she would call me the moment she got her invitation to school, but she didn't. Then I presumed her lady-in-waiting would reach out, but she didn't either. A princess who arrives in a pumpkin coach should be *begging* to work with me."

Raina pinches me, and I jump in the frame. "Hi, Marta, I'm so sorry about that! Obviously…um…I was a clueless princess who didn't read the manual and realize…um…how utterly valuable your time is and…uh…how desperately I… needed"—I look at Raina in a panic—"help."

"Devin's already had a private meeting with the headmistress," Raina says quickly. "I'm sure she will be very disappointed if she learns you couldn't give Devin an appointment until November."

At the mention of Olivina, Marta looks thoughtful. "Be down here in ten minutes." The mirror fades to black.

Raina claps excitedly and hugs me. "Move, move, move! Let's get down there!"

Brynn throws a dress over my head and drapes a sash across my torso. She points out a small pin. "Your first superlative pin is already on here. I'm so proud, miss! I'm sure you're going to add more each week."

"Sure," I say with a half-hearted smile. I'm still feeling strange about last night, but if I need to walk and talk like a princess to appease Olivina so she allows me to continue creature care, so be it. Who knows? Maybe someday I can open a fairy-tale zoo where children can see all kinds of creatures up close. Not just deer and raccoons, but unicorns and dragons! I could have a learning center and a healing center and a...

"Devin!" Sasha yells. "Let's go!"

But first I need a suitable dress.

We've been rushing through the castle so quickly that I've lost any sense of where we are. Sasha, Brynn, and Raina seem to know exactly where they're going, however, and we eventually arrive at a circular atrium. Sunlight from the glass ceiling shines down on a golden statue of Princesses Ella, Snow, Rapunzel, and Rose, but we appear to have hit a dead end. There are no windows or doors in the room.

"Is the coast clear?" Sasha asks, her eyes sharp.

"Checking." Brynn walks around the statue looking, up, down, and all around. "Clear."

Raina waves her training wand at the statue, and Sasha presses a button on Princess Ella's statue shoe. "To be ready for a ball, a princess must go to the mall."

There is a flash of light and a gust of wind, and seconds later I find myself standing in the center of a very upscale indoor market. A gold sign hanging above our heads says THE ROYAL UNDERGROUND. I recognize some of our RA classmates rushing by with bags that say SCENT-SATIONAL! and RAPUNZEL'S HAIR CARE—THE ORIGINAL SHOPPE! There's so much to see, but I'm here on a mission. I scan the shop signs around us, seeing ARABIAN NIGHTS JEWELERS (FOR ALL YOUR CROWNING NEEDS!), THE SWORD AND THE STONE, SUITS FIT FOR A PRINCE, and PINOCCHIO'S PUPPETS before spotting the sign we're looking for:

Marta Marigold
Official Dressmaker for Royal Academy
Dressing Enchantasia's Royals
for Fifteen Years!

A clock strikes nine, and Raina grabs my hand. "Don't want to be late. Come on!"

The four of us rush into the shop and find it already packed. Girls are holding up cotton-candy-colored creations and twirling on rotating pedestals. Others are looking at fabric on floating racks. There is even a mock pumpkin coach with a fake castle backdrop that princesses are using to practice entering and exiting a coach in massive skirts.

In the center of it all is Marta. Wearing a bright-green apron dotted with pins and small swatches of fabric, she is talking to one princess, pinning another, and using her wand to sew fabric to a third. A mirror above our heads flashes wait times and rules for the shop.

No questioning the tailor's judgment!

All sales are final!

If you want something different, then find a fairy godmother!

"Raina, darling, how are you?" Marta steps away from her clients. She snaps her fingers, and magic wands shoot off tables to finish the tasks she was doing for each girl. Marta air-kisses Sasha and hugs Raina. "Lovely gown you're wearing, darling. Who made that beautiful confection?"

Sasha and Raina curtsy. "You, of course!" They all laugh.

Marta turns to me, clasps my hands, and looks me straight in the eye. Her pale-blue eyes and snow-white hair remind me of my grandmother Evelyn. "This must be Princess Devin." I take Marta's hand, and she pulls me into a spin. "Let's see what I have to work with. Hmm…you've got good shoulders that can hold up a spaghetti-strap gown, that's for sure. Not too tall, not too short, with lovely arms. I'm thinking sleeveless for you. Or perhaps cap sleeves! Yes!"

"I find cap sleeves kind of binding…" I start to say, but Raina, Brynn, and Sasha shush me.

"No need to shush her," Marta tells them. "Every princess should have a unique style that suits her needs. Why, who do you think helped Rapunzel come up with those short dress hems to offset her long hair? Or gave Snow a hidden pocket that could hold a sword? Me! I've always felt a princess sparkles brightest when she is wearing something she feels

fabulous in. Step onto a pedestal, dear, and let's talk colors."
She circles me as I stand on display.

"I'm thinking green would be lovely. Maybe some dresses
in blue, perhaps. The color always worked well for Princess
Peony, one of my recent brides." She points to the wall, and I
see a wedding portrait painted with the princess, the prince,
and Marta. "For you, I'm thinking simple, understated. You
don't look like the kind of princess who enjoys too much fuss."

"I don't," I say in amazement. *Wow, she really gets people.*
Maybe I'll actually like these gowns.

"Let me gather some things, and I'll be right back to get
you started." She turns to the back wall. "*Taryn!*"

A pixie flies out of a small window in the wall with a
tiny pad.

"Clear my next two appointments. I'm going to need
time with this one."

"Yes, Marta!" the pixie says.

Raina claps. "We're definitely going to win 'best dressed
roommates' next week."

"I wouldn't be so sure about that."

I turn around. Three girls have entered behind us.
Several customers see them and scatter, and I quickly realize

why. The girl in the center looks like she wants to spit fire at me.

"Hello, Clarissa," Sasha says coolly.

Clarissa continues to stare us down. "We missed you both at the Fairy Garden Summer Solstice party."

Sasha says, "Busy," at the same time Raina says, "I was out of town."

"Olivina came," Clarissa adds. "Maybe if you had joined us, you wouldn't have been stuck with a misfit for a roommate."

"Misfit?" Sasha gets outraged before I can even think of a response. "Unorthodox, yes. Lacking in fashion sense? Possibly. But that will change with a little help from Marta and myself. More importantly, Devin is an excellent room-mate...friendly, kind, and the sort of princess who wouldn't stab you in the back the first chance she gets. She's a way better choice than you."

Whoa. Sasha is a force to be reckoned with.

Clarissa's cheeks turn crimson. "Who cares what you think? My room is the one in the *Roster*, and I'll make sure it stays that way. Have fun at your fitting, misfit." She turns and leaves the shop as dramatically as she came.

"Wow!" Raina says, giggling nervously. "I've never seen anyone go back at Clarissa before. Her family is fourth in line to the royal court, so we always tread lightly when she's around. Never know when one of them might marry someone who could challenge our rule. But you have no fear, Sasha!"

"I'm not scared of her," Sasha says, watching the girls leave.

"Thanks for sticking up for me," I say shyly. "Not that I care what that girl thinks."

"You shouldn't," Sasha replies. "She's not worth it."

My stomach growls in agreement. "How long do you think this fitting might take? We didn't stop to get breakfast first."

Sasha and Raina look at each other. "You could be here a while," Raina says.

"You need a whole wardrobe overhaul," Sasha reminds me. "These things take time. We'll get you something from Little Miss Muffin's. I could use a pumpkin muffin myself."

"Me too!" Brynn agrees, and the three of them leave, chatting.

Thump! Marta appears with a large stack of dresses and fabric swatches in shades of blues and greens. "These colors will bring out your eyes, and the fabrics are breathable and lightweight. You seem like a girl who likes to move freely. Am I right?"

"You are," I agree.

"I also think we should add some deep pockets so your little friend can be comfortable. I'll even line them with velvet so she's cozy on cold days." She waves to Lily, who just climbed onto my shoulder.

"Wow, Marta, you'd do that?" I ask. Raina was right about her being the best.

"Darling, I may be tough to get an appointment with, but stick with me, and you'll be just fine! I decide on the colors and fabrics, and you look gorgeous and represent *moi*. It's a win-win."

She begins to hum to herself as she holds up swatches. A thought comes to me, but I hesitate to bring it up. I'm not sure if Marta will go for it. She does seem like a trail-blazer though. "Marta? I have an idea. It's a little different, but something I always thought would be amazing in case of emergencies." I clear my throat. "I think it will look really, um, fashion-forward too."

Marta looks up. "Yes, darling? What is it."

I look around, then bend down so that I'm sure only she can hear. "Have you ever stitched pants under dress skirts? So that they're hidden?"

"Pants?" she repeats, mulling it over.

"They're so comfortable, and you never know when a princess might have to break into a run to avoid danger. You would be helping a new generation of princesses escape evil! We could even give the pants a name, like 'the Marta.'"

"The Marta," she repeats, transfixed. "Darling! It's brilliant! Why have I never thought of it before now?" She talks fast. "I'm thinking light cotton so you're not too hot, with a breakaway skirt so that you can rip it off if it gets in the way, in a stand-out pattern to give the look punch, should you ever lose your skirt." She closes her eyes and thinks. "I see the pants in purple! Yes! With white polka dots."

"I like it!" I nod.

"This will be exciting. Pants! The Marta. And it will be our secret for now."

I reach out and hug her. "Marta, I feel like you get me."

"I do! Let me go get more material!" she says excitedly. "Stay right there!"

For the first time in my life, I'm excited about a dress.

"Looking for an outfit that will wow me?"

I turn to see Heath leaning against the doorway, giving me a smile so bright that two of the pixies working in the shop see him and faint. He's wearing his RA sash over a gray double-breasted coat and black pants, and his high black boots shine like they've just been polished. I can't help thinking that Marta would approve. A group of girls hovers in the doorway, watching him.

"Nope. I'm getting dresses that will wow *me*," I say pointedly.

"Good for you. I was just getting a haircut." He touches his short locks, and I hear a girl sigh. His hair looks the same as it did yesterday. "Then I stopped at Little Miss Muffin to order some bagels and Goldie Lox and heard you were with Marta, so I thought I'd stop by and make your morning."

I roll my eyes. "Is this what you do all day? Just go around stroking your ego and annoying unsuspecting students?"

He holds his heart. "That hurts. I do other stuff too!"

"Oh yeah." I snort. "Like ditching class to go climbing with knights-in-training at Mount Hibesko." Raina told me all about it.

"Okay, yeah, I did that, but only because I'd never been and I like to explore," he says, and I'm surprised to hear defensiveness in his voice. "My plan is to see all the kingdoms in the realm before I'm twenty. Then…I don't know." His cheeks brighten. "I thought maybe I could write a series of scrolls about the people and places I've seen. A lot of people don't get to travel, so I thought I could be their eyes."

I'm dumbfounded. That actually sounds cool. "I think people would love that."

He leans against the carriage and looks off in the direction of Goose Girl Gowns. "But who am I kidding? My parents will have me married off before I get to do any of that."

"Then don't let them!" I say passionately. "I think letting the people read about places they'll never get to see is an amazing idea."

"You think so?" Heath says softly, moving closer to my pedestal.

"I do." The two of us look at each other.

"Oh, look at that!" Marta coos, startling us. "I've made a prince and princess match already and haven't even finished her dress yet!"

"Oh we're not… He's not… I mean, we're not…" I stutter.

Heath regains his swagger as he walks out of the shop. "Tell yourself what you want, blondie." And with a wink, he's gone.

ROYAL ACADEMY

Schedule for First-Year Princesses

Section A

1. Creature Comfort with Princess Snow (New this year!)

2. History of Enchantasia with Professor Pierce

3. Lunch or beauty touch-up! (Royal Underground lip-staining sessions are first come, first served.)

4. *Embracing Your Inner Princess with Olivina (Please note, Olivina's fairy godmother duties prevent her from one-on-one conversations during class times.)

5. You may attend either of the following electives during fifth period:

From Cha-Chas to Charming Princes: Dance Lessons with Madame Rosalinda

Princess Hair Care with Hazel (Tiaras will be available for use in class. No need to bring your own. Additional styles will be available for purchase!)

6. How to Write (a Love Note) with Professor Carrington

◇◇◇◇◇◇◇

Embracing Your Inner Princess will not meet this week. Instead, enjoy daily meet-ups with the princes!

Class times, schedule, and special events change on a daily basis. Please consult your scrolls to learn more.

CHAPTER 13

SNOW'S CLASS

I had no idea we'd have different classes than the boys!" Raina freaks as she reads the scroll containing her schedule.

"Are you really surprised?" Sasha asks, taking notes on her scroll. "Our required reading lists were totally different. Didn't you ever look at Heath's?"

Raina slips on a pair of long white gloves. "Who had the time? I was busy pulling together my wardrobe." She places her RA sash over her head and lays it on top of her pale-pink dress. "How are we going to meet a prince if we aren't even with them half the day?"

"We have *some* classes with the boys," I point out optimistically. "I'm sure we'll be fine. But it looks like our schedules are different. Sasha and I have your sister's class in the morning, and you don't have it until the afternoon."

Raina snatches my schedule out of my hands and compares it to hers. "Why would they separate us? Ugh, I better not have all my classes with Clarissa. Well, I suppose we'll just have to wait to meet up until afternoon tea, then."

I'm feeling Raina's panic too, but for a different reason. Snow's class is happening! And I'm in it! But the rest of my schedule looks wonky. How to write a love note? From cha-chas to charming princes? Why should the boys be the only ones who learn how to slay a giant or a dragon? Where are the classes that are supposed to teach us how to rule a kingdom? Lily flicks her tongue at me as if to say "too bad!" And she's right, I guess. I promised Olivina I would behave like a princess, and a real princess would love the classes I got...I think.

I glance in the mirror and attempt to straighten my tiara. I try not to think about how it is pinching my skull. I slip into my not-very-comfortable but Marta-approved shoes, and smooth out the creases in my pale-green organza dress, taking some satisfaction in the fact that it has a hidden pair of pants underneath.

(I have to hand it to Marta. When she goes for a trend,

she goes all in. She put purple polka-dot pants in all my gowns and promised we'd keep the secret just between us.)

It's showtime.

"You're so lucky, miss!" Brynn looks over my scroll. "This schedule seems wonderful!"

Now I feel guilty for even wanting to complain. Brynn wants to take classes so badly. "I'll share all my notes with you after class tonight," I whisper in her ear as she snaps a pearl necklace around my neck. Brynn beams.

"I'm skipping today's meet-up," Sasha says. "I've got to finish the *Enchantasia Insider*, and I want to get it out tonight. I only got four hours of beauty sleep last night. There's still so much to write and edit. And besides, any prince that wants to meet me should have to work to find me."

"Is that allowed?" I ask hurriedly. "If so, I think I'll skip too." I don't really feel like mingling with princes today.

"I think so," Sasha says. "Did you guys see Olivina's class was canceled for today? How could she miss her first day?"

My chest tightens at the sound of Olivina's name. Sasha looks at me strangely, and I realize I'm biting my strand of pearls.

"Oh, Sasha, stop being all sleuthy." Raina takes off the gloves and adds a few beaded bracelets to her arms instead.

"Olivina is a busy fairy godmother! I'm sure she's just off granting some all-important wishes that couldn't wait."

"Maybe," Sasha says, but I can see the wheels in her writer brain working.

I'm not saying a word. "How do I look?" I ask the group.

"Like a future queen!" Milo's mirror has come alive in a swirl of gold and silver. I jump at his voice. I forgot someone is always watching here. "Remember...to wear a crown, you have to not just look the part, you have to follow the protocol set forth for someone of your stature. Put your best slippered heel forward!" The mirror's glow goes dark.

Raina ties a bow atop her head and smiles. "I can tell this is going to be a great first day. Now let's get going. I want to be first to class. Remember: the early princess gets the prince!"

Even after studying a map, I see the castle is bigger than I realized. A wrong turn can land you in any number of rooms. I already accidentally walked into an incredibly elaborate powder room that reminded me of Mirror Image, a beauty store in Enchantasia, and a full-blown armory.

It doesn't help that the hallways are so crowded. I keep getting bumped by princes carrying gear to their first class (Brute Strength: Practice Makes Prince Perfect!) and princesses heading to primping sessions in the Royal Underground. Eventually, we find our way to Snow's classroom, which has horse posts outside the large double doors. Excitedly, I head inside and find... *wow!*

There are two aisles of pens and cages filled with very vocal animals. I spot a cougar, a leopard, and a ball python kept separate from horses and a flock of geese. In the center of the room, Princess Snow is busy setting things out at a large table. She's got snacks and bandages, and look! There's even a tiny stethoscope. This is exactly what I was hoping for! She sees me and waves me over.

"Hi, Devin. Excited about today's first class? I know I am." Snow's dark eyes are hopeful. "I've wanted to teach a class like this for so long! I just hope the students are open to learning. I've already had a gentleman tell me that he's allergic to dragons."

Logan. I don't see him. Maybe I should start checking under the tables. "I think he'll be okay."

Snow nods. "I just want things to go well so we can keep this class and add others like it. The royals have to keep moving forward, as Professor Pierce and I like to say." She half smiles. "And I have such great creatures to introduce you all to."

A carrier pigeon dives low, almost nailing me in the head, and drops a rolled parchment on the table. Before flying off, he looks at me and coos. *That woman is crazy!*

What woman? I want to ask.

Snow reads the parchment and frowns. "Oh. But… well…" Snow sighs. "This certainly changes things," she says. I catch a glimpse of the signature before she folds the note and slips it in her apron. It's from Olivina. "If you'll excuse me, I should start class."

I wonder what that was about. No matter. Class is starting! I take my place next to Sasha, who is with a group of princesses standing next to a pen of baby goats.

Snow claps her hands. "Hello, everyone! As you know, Creature Comfort is a new course I'm proud to introduce this year. I don't want anyone to be nervous," she adds, glancing Logan's way. (He didn't bail after all!) "It's my goal for each of you to become more comfortable around our animal counterparts. They've been wonderful friends to me, and they can be the same for you. Any animal can be a help, from the largest rhino to the smallest bumblebee."

"A bumblebee?" A prince and his friends burst out laughing.

I glare at them. "Bumblebees are really smart," I say. "Did

you know they can see color? And they can even do tricks. I once taught one to roll a ball."

"Roll a ball?" The prince looks skeptical. "Please stop talking, blondie."

Sasha touches my arm. "Ignore him," she whispers. "Derek Hoffstater's older brother dated my first cousin, and the whole family is pompous. Don't engage."

I bite my tongue.

"Thank you, Devin," Professor Snow says gently. "Now, I know this class is coed, but it has just been decided that princes and princesses will be split up for different exercises." Snow smiles apologetically.

Come again?

"Girls, you're going to stay where you are, while the boys will be working on our secret project, which is down the hall in our meet-and-greet animal room."

"Meet-and-greet?" Logan looks at me pleadingly.

"It will be quite enlightening. Follow me," says Snow, looking uncomfortable. "Girls, if you wouldn't mind each getting a bowl of pine nuts ready, we'll use them when I come back."

I look at Sasha. "They get to do a secret project in the animal meet-and-greet room, and we get pine nuts?" I grumble.

"I'm sure we're using the same animals," Sasha says, but I'm not convinced, especially when Snow returns with a small box.

Snow makes eye contact quickly with me. "Now, this wasn't scheduled, but I'm sure it will still be fun. Presenting your first animal friend…the chipmunk!"

"Awww," chorus the princesses.

The chipmunk? I'm offended. So is the chipmunk, who makes a small chittering sound. *What's up with this crowd? Know where I can find a good pine nut?*

"What's he saying?" Sasha asks me, but I'm too annoyed to answer her.

Neither the chipmunk nor I are any happier when we learn today's "skill" is learning how to make our animal friend feel comfortable enough to crawl onto our skirts. Chipmunks are notoriously not cuddlers, even when they like you. And princesses are notoriously not known for activities where they can be pooped on. But, at Snow's bidding, the princesses reluctantly get down on the floor, cooing and smiling at the chipmunks to try to entice them to come closer—with varying degrees of success. Next, Snow shows us how to get our chipmunks to eat a pine nut out of our palms.

"Can you tell mine to sit on my lap, at least," Sasha

complains as she waves the nut wildly at her chipmunk. "I don't want to fail my first assignment."

"I told you. Move slowly and ask nicely. Chipmunks appreciate your patience, and they love people who are very calm," I tell her. My chipmunk is sitting on my shoulder.

Sasha tries bird noises, catcalls, and even a few neighs to try to get the chipmunk's attention, but he won't budge. Her chipmunk looks at mine and chitters, *And they said this class would be fun? I'm bored.*

Me too, I want to tell them. All we're learning today is how to feed a chipmunk? I look at Snow, who is going from princess to princess and giving advice. Every few minutes she runs back to the other room. I can hear loud talking coming from down the hall, and I'm so curious...and jealous. Is this really what she had planned for us today?

"What are the boys doing anyway?" I ask Sasha. If only I could see!

Sasha shrugs. "No clue. Maybe it's dangerous. Why don't you ask the chipmunk? Maybe he knows."

The chipmunk looks at me. *No clue.*

"He doesn't know. And besides, dangerous? Creature Comfort?" I start to laugh.

Thump.

Thump.

The ground beneath us starts to shake. The glasses on Snow's desk start to move. A vial of beet juice shatters on the floor. Animals in the pens get restless. The cougar lets out a low growl. Okay, maybe I shouldn't have laughed at that dangerous part. What are the princes doing down there?

"Students, if you will just excuse me for a second…" Snow starts to say, but she's drowned out by a loud roar.

I inhale sharply, half-excited, half-terrified as I smell a hint of smoke in the air. "Dragon," I whisper.

"Dragon?" Sasha repeats as we hear a commotion down the hall.

Both of our chipmunks hear this and start to run. *I'm out of here!* they chatter.

The boys' room bursts open and princes come flooding out, some screaming. Logan is leading the pack.

"Derek let the dragon loose!" Logan shouts. "*Run!*"

He dives under a desk seconds before a giant, greenish-gray beast bursts through the double doors behind him. His eyes are red and wild as his head searches left, then right, for what I assume is the exit.

"Loose?" Snow cries. "You were supposed to study the eggs. Not engage with the dragon yet! That's an upper-level skill! Why did Olivina suggest a dragon on day one?" I hear her mutter.

All I can do is stare in awe as others take off running. The dragon is the most beautiful creature I've ever seen! Its scales are almost translucent and its wings so expansive that I'm sure at full width they could cover the entire room. One claw is the size of my whole body, and the tail might be the length of my dorm room. I should be scared, but instead my mind is racing with questions. Where does it call home? How do dragons store up enough fiery breath to take out a whole village?

"Devin, let's go!" Sasha calls, snapping me out of my fog. "You are not trying to talk to that thing!" The girls around me almost trample their chipmunks in their quest to get to the exit. Students stream into the hallways screaming "Dragon! Dragon!" I sweep a bunch of chipmunks up in my arms and place them back in their box, then close the lid just to be safe.

Click! Click! Click! Snow is moving slowly toward the dragon while making a clucking sound with her tongue.

The dragon stops walking around long enough to look at her.

"It's okay. Come with me now," she coaxes.

Thump! It whacks its large tail against the floor.

I hold my breath and wait for the fire to start, but the dragon ignores Snow. He's searching and sniffing alcoves. One contains the horses, who start to neigh furiously. A steed breaks from its holding, galloping down the aisle and out the classroom doors, distracting the dragon and sending students diving out of the way.

"Come on, men!" says Derek. "Let's get this beast back into its cage. Draw your swords!"

"Don't hurt him!" Snow cries. "He's just scared. Stay back! I can control him!"

"*Charge!*" Milo's voice booms from a mirror in the room. "Charge, young princes! The headmistress demands you step up and send this creature back to its holdings."

"No!" Snow protests.

"And you, Professor Snow, should plan on having a meeting with the headmistress when this situation is contained," Milo snaps. "It's obvious this class is way too dangerous for our young royals."

"This was an accident!" Snow protests, arguing with… um…the mirror. "We weren't even supposed to study dragons today! All the students were supposed to meet unicorns! Olivina made the switch. I certainly wouldn't have suggested a creature like a dragon, who could cause damage when let loose."

"That is all," says Milo. "The princes will deal with this." His mirror goes dark, and the dragon roars again.

Sasha pulls me into an empty alcove. "The nerve of him, telling Snow what she can and can't do!"

"You heard her!" I seethe. "We weren't even supposed to meet a dragon today. What is Olivina doing?"

"Devin!" Logan comes sliding toward me, staying low and ducking so the dragon doesn't spot him. He's out of breath. "The dragon. I can't believe I'm—*Achoo!*—saying this, but it's not—*Achoo!*—its fault!"

"What do you mean?" I whisper as the dragon begins cawing like it's calling for someone. Another dragon? The call sounds desperate, but I can't understand dragon.

"Derek didn't just let the dragon out. He stole one of the dragon's eggs!" Logan tells me. "He was saying something about it being worth a ton of gold. He took one, and the dragon saw. That's when he burst out. I think he's looking for it."

Of course! The dad dragon is looking for his baby! His

157

caws are getting more and more desperate. So are the actions of the princes. They brandish their swords at the dragon, coming close to nicking his skin. This only agitates the creature more.

"We have to find that egg," I say. "But we can't let the dragon leave this room. He could end up hurting people." I can't say this for certain of all dragons, but this one doesn't seem interested in hurting anyone. *Yet.*

"I'll find the egg," Sasha volunteers. "Logan, help me find Derek. He can't be far."

"Oh, I—*Achoo!*—can't," Logan says. "I'm allergic."

"To dragon eggs?" Sasha asks. "We have to get that egg back, or the dragon will rip the school apart looking for its baby!" She grabs his hand, giving him no choice. "Now come on!"

"I'll stay here and hold the dragon off," I say. "Go quickly!"

ROAAARRR! The dragon knocks over two bookcases, and Snow and the few remaining students in the room start to scatter. One of the princes pokes the dragon hard, and it screeches.

"Back away from that dragon!" I shout, and everyone looks at me.

The prince nudges me with his sword. "You back up, princess. This isn't a job for you."

I narrow my eyes at him.

"Devin, wait!" Snow warns, but I ignore her.

"It is if you keep screwing up!" I pull the sword out of his hand. The princes around him gasp. "*You* back up. You're scaring him! It's only going to make things worse."

"This is not your jurisdiction, princess," says another prince.

It's clear I'm not going to get any help from the guys. I have to try to help the dragon on my own. "Are you looking for your baby? Your egg?" I ask the creature. "Don't worry! We're going to bring it back to you. We just need you to stay calm and wait."

"Devin, you can't!" Snow sounds frantic. "I know it's hard to sit back, but let the princes find this egg if that's what's really going on. It's their job." I open my mouth to protest. "They'll restrain the dragon. *Please!* I can't let this happen to another student, not after Tara…"

I'm about to ask, "Who's Tara?" when the dragon bounds in front of me and cocks its head like it's listening to what I have to say. His face comes dangerously close to mine. "Nice dragon," I say, trying not to sound frightened. Just one of his teeth is as big as my head.

"It's going to attack Princess Devin!" The first prince grabs another boy's dagger and stabs it into the dragon's tail.

The dragon roars so loudly that the ground shakes violently. Seconds later, it opens its mouth.

"*Duck!*" I cry as fire rains down on the room.

Snow's table is the first casualty. Two pixies race into the room to put the fire out with mini magical sparkles, but the dragon is still breathing fire. The princes dive at the dragon.

"No!" I cry again.

"Devin! We have it!" Sasha holds the egg high above her head as she races back into class. Logan is right behind her, grinning triumphantly. "We have the egg! Logan hit Derek! You should have seen... *Oh!*" She screams as fire shoots in her direction.

The dragon thinks Sasha stole the egg! "Sasha!" I run toward her. "Put the egg down and back away. No one move!"

Sasha gently places the egg on the floor, then walks backward slowly till she's next to me. We hold our breaths.

The dragon sniffs the egg, poking it with his nose before carefully picking it up with his teeth. He snorts in my direction, and I have to imagine he's thanking us.

We watch as he heads back the way he came. Snow hurries after the dragon to lock him up. She looks back at me worriedly, but I'm smiling. I met a real live dragon!

"You guys did it!" I hug Logan and Sasha.

"We *all* did!" Logan says with a laugh. "I hit a prince and spoke to a dragon and—*Achoo!*—I'm still alive!"

Sasha starts to laugh too. "And I helped save the day! Wow, that felt good!"

Then we hear a voice behind us.

"Miss Devin, Miss Sasha, and Mr. Logan!" Hazel is out of breath as she clings to what's left of our door. She looks furious as she looks around at the charred remains of our classroom. "You…you…you three are in *major* trouble."

ROYAL ACADEMY

From the desk of the Fairy Godmother

Devin,

I thought we had an understanding, but after hearing—and seeing—what happened in Professor Snow's class, I fear I was wrong. Not only did you speak out of turn and handle things in a matter unbecoming of a princess, but you also corrupted Sasha Briarwood and Logan Nederlander. They have each received a strike because of <u>you</u>. And that's to say nothing of the other students who witnessed how the three of you handled the situation.

I regret to inform you that your parents have been made aware of this infraction. For now, the news will stay quiet, but if word of your poor performance were to get out to other royal families, the shame your parents would feel would be dreadful. I'd hate to see your behavior affect your father's chance to earn lead commander ranking in the Royal Infantry. This is strike two. You do not want to get a third.

I really hope you can turn things around. There is so much I want to teach you and discuss with you once I know you can be trusted. I know if you want to badly enough, you can do anything!

Forever yours in wishes,

Headmistress Olivina

FAIRY-TALE MYTHS

I am on strike two.

My hands are shaking, and my legs feel like jelly as I read the letter. The bells are signaling we need to get to our next class, but I can't breathe. If I screw up again, not only will I be banished, but Father and Mother's lives will be ruined. Father's Royal Infantry career could be over. I can't let that happen. The class bell tolls again, and I look up to see an enraged Sasha marching toward me.

She shakily holds up a scroll identical to my own, and I pale. "Not only did I get a strike, but the Fairy Godmother told me I can't publish my next issue of the *Enchantasia Insider!*" Her eyes are rimmed with tears. "She said she knew I was the author and that I'd shown poor judgment in writing about what happened at First Knight Out. Anything that happens at Royal Academy is off-limits, which infringes on my freedom of speech. She never would have started with me if I hadn't helped you with that dragon!"

"Sasha, I'm so sorry—" I start to say, but she cuts me off.

"If I continue to be friends with you and follow your ways, Olivina said she'll throw me out and tell the world I couldn't cut it as a princess." Her expression darkens. "I can't let that happen. My family can't take that kind of scandal. Not after my sister…"

I blink rapidly. "Olivina said that?" I'm shocked. I didn't think fairy godmothers said such things. "But we're roommates."

"Just stay away from me, okay?" Sasha backs away, banging into Clarissa and a few of her friends. "Stay far, far away!"

I'm so caught up, I forget we have an audience. I can feel everyone's eyes on me. Clarissa smirks, while a few princesses whisper and stare. I am not sure where to turn. It feels like the walls of the castle are closing in, and all I want to do is run. When the second bell rings, that's just what I do. I don't stop till I reach Professor Pierce's classroom.

I slide into the first chair I see and stare at my desk, willing myself not to cry. *Sasha's scroll is in jeopardy. Father's career might be ruined. Mother will never be able to show her face at the charity Enchantasia Mad Tea Party again. What have I done? It's only the first week, and already I'm close to losing everything.*

"Good morning to the future of Enchantasia!"

I look up curiously. Professor Pierce's smile is magnanimous. Something about it makes my heart rate slow to normal again. All around me, people stop talking and just smile. I'm not sure what it is about him. He's dressed pretty regally for a teacher—in a royal-blue double-breasted dress coat and gold pants—which is impressive. But there is just something about his kind eyes—which are a unique shade of gray—that make me feel like everything is going to be okay.

"Who's ready to help change the world?" he asks, walking toward our desks. People sit up straighter to listen. "I know I am, and I know you are too. As royals, that's your duty. To help make people's lives better and brighter, and I hope in this room you will learn to do that. There's only one rule in here: Be honest. Honesty is important in a royal—in all humans—and I want you to know that Milo will never make an appearance in this room. You can speak freely."

"Headmistress Olivina allows that?" It's Clarissa's best friend, Morticia Von Meader. She sounds nervous even asking the question.

"Absolutely!" says Professor Pierce. "This is actually part of an agreement the fairy godmother and I made in exchange for me teaching here. This classroom is a safe space." I could swear he looks at me. "And with that, we are going to dive into today's lesson." He taps the board, which ripples like water, and words appear in tight, neat script.

The History of Enchantasia

"To understand how to serve as a ruler, we must first study the royals who have ruled throughout history, examining their successes and their failures," he explains.

Professor Pierce taps the board again, and an image of Princess Ella appears, as clear as if she were standing right in front of us. The class gasps. More images come into view. Beauty, from her and Prince Sebastian's story, imprisoned; Snow lying in what appears to be an eternal sleep, much like Princess Rose. The famous faces fly by.

"The headmistress and I have always agreed we shouldn't shy away from the tough side of being royal. In fact, she has always encouraged me to explore the dangers you may face on the road to the throne." His smile is thin. "But ruling isn't just about dramatic rescues and ceremonial gatherings. Being royal means acting responsibly with the power that you're given. It's about making tough decisions for the good of your subjects. I hope my class will help you to do so." He taps the board again, and it fades to black.

The classroom is quiet. All eyes are on Professor Pierce.

"Who can tell me some of the hardships royals have faced?" he asks.

A flurry of hands shoot up, and students recount stories we all know. Tales of Princess Ella and Headmistress Flora, the former Wicked Stepmother. Snow and the Evil Queen. The Little Mermaid and Madame Cleo, the sea siren. Rapunzel and Gottie. Wow, there have been a lot more villain attacks in our kingdom than I realized. This discussion is getting sort of depressing.

"Why would anyone want to rule, knowing villains are always waiting to attack?" Logan asks, reading my thoughts.

"That's a good point, Mr. Nederlander," the professor says. "But as Olivina will remind you, this isn't a job you signed up for. It is one you were born into and are expected to carry out. Still, I think it's important we figure out how to deal with threats to our kingdoms."

"Olivina always helps us do that!" one girl says, and the others nod.

A prince in the back of the class raises his hand.

"Yes, Mr. Wallington?"

"What about regular thieves and criminals? I remember King John dealt with a commoner who was stealing all his gold and handing it out *for free*. King John had to launch a task force, but he couldn't find the thief."

Professor Pierce looks thoughtful. "Ah yes, Robin Hood. That's an interesting one. It could be said that Robin Hood was stealing from the king. But King John was later relieved of his royal status when he was discovered to be unlawfully taxing the commoners to add to his personal fortune. So who's to say who's right? King John, who made harmful decisions for his people but was the true ruler of the kingdom, or Robin Hood, who technically broke the law but did it in service to the people? It's an interesting case that shows the complexities behind determining what is wrong and what is right. We can't forget that, while it is fruitful to study famous cases involving royals, commoners can often teach us much as well."

Clarissa scoffs, and Professor Pierce raises his eyebrows.

"It seems that Miss Hartworth would disagree. Can

anyone think of a famous commoner from whom we can learn something?"

The room is quiet, except for the noise of shifting chairs and rustling papers. I take a deep breath and raise my hand. The professor nods for me to speak. "What about Red Riding Hood?"

Professor Pierce smiles. "Very good, Miss Nile."

He taps his board, and a girl in a red cloak appears, standing in the woods with a bow and arrow. "When a wolf threatened her safety, Red took matters into her own hands."

"But we're supposed to wait for help," a girl in the back row pipes up. "Aren't we?"

We all look at our teacher. "Yes, that is the headmistress's preferred approach." Professor Pierce is quiet for a moment. "But if Red had followed convention, she wouldn't be where she is today. Not only did Red stop the wolf, but she also grew stronger and more powerful than anyone could imagine. Today, she owns a readiness and preparedness shop in Enchantasia Village, and she is one of the most sought-after huntresses in the Hollow Woods. Even though it was hard, she overcame her adversity and used it to help others empower themselves. And if that's not a lesson we can apply to life as a royal, I'm not sure what is."

The two of us make eye contact. I know it's silly, but a part of me feels like he's talking directly to me. And for the first time since arriving at RA, I'm feeling inspired.

TEATIME

As much as I like finger sandwiches, the last thing I want to do this afternoon is have tea. Not even those swan-shaped cream puffs could make me want to sit at a table with my roommates right now.

"Hello, miss!" says Brynn, appearing at my side as I stand at the entrance to the banquet hall. She guides me into the room and steers me toward my table. "How were your classes this morning? Good? I heard Professor Pierce's history class is the most enlightening of all first-year studies. Maybe I could look at your notes later. I've always wanted to learn more about the ogre uprising. I've always thought if the royals had just met with the ogre king before the troll bridge collapsed, all that fighting could have been avoided. Don't you agree?"

"Uh-huh." My eyes are on a table across the room where Sasha and Raina are sitting together, talking quietly. I look around frantically for somewhere else to sit, scanning the elaborately decorated room. Candelabras are on all the tables, which are set with orange china for the first day of fall, and a violinist is serenading us with classical music. My eyes land on Clarissa, who has added three pillows to her velvet-lined chair because she's so tiny. I'm definitely not approaching her table. And there is no way I want to sit with that table of princes who are using their knives as swords. Brynn and the other ladies-in-waiting eat in an adjacent banquet hall, separate from young royals, and Logan is nowhere to be seen.

"I'm actually not feeling too well," I say as I see Raina waving while Sasha pointedly refuses to look at me. "I think I'll just go back to my room for a spell and…uh…nap."

"Nap?" Brynn repeats. "Miss, I didn't know you to be a napper."

I'm not. I'm a terrible sleeper, actually. Brynn knows this.

"Though, you do look a little pale." Brynn smiles and takes my arm. "A cup of tea will do you good! I already ordered your favorite—green peppermint. Now, come on. Raina and Sasha are saving a seat for you."

Brynn is leading me to the table before I can stop her.

She pulls out the chair and plops me in it. "I'll have your teapot sent right over, miss. As you can see, the finger foods have just arrived."

I resist the urge to reach out and grab Brynn's arm to force her to stay. Instead, I put my napkin on my lap and try to remember which fork I'm supposed to use to take some strawberries. I grab a cream puff swan to calm my nerves and stuff it in my mouth.

"Hi," I mumble.

"Hi," Raina says pleasantly. "I was just telling Sasha about how I *accidentally* knocked Amber's tiara off during Cha-Chas to Charming Princes this morning. No way she's getting Best Dressed again this week on the superlatives!" She wipes her mouth with her napkin daintily. "How were your classes this morning?" She looks at me expectantly, and I glance nervously at Sasha.

If looks were curses, Sasha's would have just turned me into a frog. "They were an absolute nightmare."

"I wasn't trying to get you in trouble," I blurt out. "I had no idea helping a dragon reunite with its baby egg would give us a strike. I really thought we did the right thing!"

"Maybe we did, but I shouldn't have gotten so caught up in your shenanigans!" Sasha says angrily, and I'm not sure who she's really mad at—me or herself. "I can't afford to get another strike. I *have* to stay at RA. I have plans that are already in motion, and they're only going to work out if I'm in the actual school."

I'm too afraid to ask what she's talking about.

A pixie flies over our table with questions. "Creamer? Soy milk? Sugar?" She keeps going when we don't answer her. "How rude," she mumbles.

"You got a *strike*?" Raina looks alarmed. "Why? When did you get a strike?" She looks from Sasha to me and back again.

"This morning in your sister's class," Sasha says. She's looking at Raina but talking to me. "Snow asked us to stay out of it when a dragon got loose, but Devin decided we should help the dragon since she can talk to it, and Olivina got mad we didn't let the princes handle it."

"I never said I could talk to dragons," I point out. "I only said I'd try."

"Why would you be so foolish?" Raina demands, pounding her fist and making our china teacups wobble. "Do you know how damaging a strike can be?"

"It's not good," I say, looking at the serving plate again to see if there is another swan cream puff. My face is flaming. "I know." This conversation is depressing.

"We should be on the superlative list together as best roomies, not the roommates with the most strikes!" Her voice is shrill.

"Raina, relax," Sasha says, taking a sip of tea with her pinkie pointed straight in the air. "It's not like you got a strike too."

"It's guilt by association!" Raina waves a paper fan over her face to calm herself down. "Everyone will be talking about how you both have strikes, which turns into everyone talking about how the royal court's siblings have strikes! Amber Arnold is going to have a field day!"

"That's what you're worried about?" Sasha snaps. "What Amber Arnold thinks? My entire life's work is in jeopardy right now!"

"What about *my* life's work of preparing to be a successful and beloved royal?" Raina is becoming hysterical. "Nothing is going the way it's supposed to here! I was supposed to be at the top of the superlatives and get invited to private teas with Olivina like Snow once was. My name was supposed to open doors. Instead, the only person I can get an appointment with is Marta, and I'm sure that's because my sister called her!" She's hyperventilating. "You two have to stop misbehaving!"

"I'm not misbehaving! This is all Devin's fault!" Sasha bites back.

"I'm sorry, okay?" I say, throwing down the last of my (*cough*) third cream puff. "I'm not trying to get in trouble. I'm just… I don't know, being myself! Is that so wrong?"

"It is if it goes against everything a princess is supposed to stand for!" Raina freaks out.

"You just have to play along," Sasha tells me heatedly. "Even if you don't agree. Fake it till you make it!"

"Follow the manual!" Raina throws the book down on the table, and a pixie gasps. "It's not hard! Just read the manual and follow it." Raina has a wild look in her eyes I've never seen before. But before I can say anything else, we're interrupted.

"Hey!" Logan slides into a seat at our table along with Heath. "I heard they have olive focaccia finger sandwiches today. Personally, if I was making them, I would have opted for ham cornbread sandwiches. I made those all the time for Mother when Father and my brothers were out giant-hunting." He looks at our faces and pauses. "Did I interrupt something?"

"You all look mad!" Heath sounds amused. "What's this

about? Does one of you need to talk? Because I'm a good listener." He bats his eyes, and Raina smacks him.

"These two are ruining my RA experience!" she tells Heath.

"Oh, Raina, please!" Sasha counters.

Swoop! A group of pixies fly by, and one drops a scroll right into Raina's lap. It's tied with a simple red ribbon, and the handwriting on the outside looks uncomfortably familiar.

Raina unrolls it and reads it quickly. Her face pales. She lets the paper flutter to the floor and points a shaky finger in my direction. "I think you should leave."

I'm one bite into a cucumber dill sandwich. "Me?" The crumbs fall as I talk. "What did I do now?"

"That scroll is from Olivina," she whispers hotly. "She said I should stay away from you! That you could be a bad influence."

"That's what she said to me too," Sasha seconds. My tea sandwich softens from the sweat on my hands.

"If I want to stay the course at RA, she's advising I distance myself from trouble until you can find your way," Raina adds, then covers her mouth. "I'm not sure I was supposed to actually relay that."

"Devin, trouble?" Logan repeats. "I got a warning, but that's not Devin's fault. Besides, I'd do the same thing again.

That dragon just wanted his baby back. Anyone could see that. And if I'm sticking up for a dragon, you know it must be true. I hate dragons!"

"Rai, calm down," Heath tells her. "It's just a warning. Father gave them to me all the time. Nothing ever came of them."

"I don't want a warning!" Raina cries, standing up quickly and throwing her napkin on her chair. "I want everything to be exactly how it should be!" She's shouting now, and everyone in the banquet hall is turning to stare. "And you're ruining that, Devin Nile! If you hate Royal Academy so much, why did you even come here?"

Because I wasn't given a choice, I think.

Raina turns and runs out of the room, sobbing. With a sigh, Heath drops what's left of his brownie, shrugs, and takes off after her. Sasha gets up quietly from the table and pushes in her chair too.

As she walks away, I'm left wondering what Olivina will do next. All I know is I don't want to find out. It's time to fall in line.

IN MY IVORY TOWER

*G*ood morning, Royal Academy! How to Pose Like a Proper Princess has been canceled today. Instead, we will be having a Getting to Know You social complete with a visit from Cobbler Shoes, Enchantasia's number one shoemaker! They're now taking orders for gold slippers, so don't miss out on this fun event!

Good afternoon, Royal Academy! Since the weather looks stormy, Professor Pierce's field trip to observe princess politics in action at the royal court's town hall meeting has been canceled. Instead, consider joining your classmates for an impromptu dance party *with Monsieur Andre, who will be teaching How to Dance Your Way into Royalty's Heart.*

Happy Friday, Royal Academy! Who is excited for this weekend's September Social? The bake sale at the RA rugby match against Fairy Tale Reform School will benefit the Save Humpty Dumpty Foundation. And not to worry—FTRS has assured us all their baked goods are hex-free and safe for consumption. Please note Headmistress Olivina was called away on official RA business so her Royal Studies class is canceled. Enjoy your free time getting ready for this weekend's festivities!

"Again?" I ask as Logan and I wind our way around the castle past a group of girls making wishes in a well. "Do you think it's weird we haven't had her class once yet?" In all honesty, I'm relieved I haven't had to see Olivina since she sent the scrolls to Sasha and Raina last week. But that doesn't make her continued absence any less peculiar.

"It is kind of strange," Logan agrees.

The two of us have been spending a lot of time together,

especially now that I'm avoiding my dorm room. And that was before the latest *Roster* came out. I can't imagine how Raina and Sasha reacted to none of us being on the list. Thankfully, I have Logan. Even though he also got a strike after what went down in Snow's class, he wasn't mad at me. ("I think it makes me look kind of manly," he said.)

"But everyone says this is normal," he adds. "Olivina has always spent more time out of RA than in it. Apparently, last week she was only here one day!" He dodges a pixie. "She's so busy. Between sitting in on all meetings with the royal court and scouting new up-and-coming royal talent, I have no clue how she has enough time to run a school."

"Maybe fairy godmothers don't need sleep," I joke. "She really does a lot. The only time I've even seen her sit still was when…I was called to her quarters and given my first strike. And then I got another because of the dragon incident." I glance at Logan worriedly. "I'm still really sorry about that strike."

Logan shrugs. "It's only one. Between us, I still think how we handled everything in Snow's class was the right way. Even if it means I can't go to my culinary class anymore."

"What?" I stop short and almost bang into a pack of pixies going in the opposite direction. "You didn't tell me that."

"You were already so upset about your roommates," he says. "I didn't want to upset you more. It's okay. I'm sure she'll let me back in the class eventually."

I don't believe that, but I keep silent.

"I meant to ask you… Did you ever ask Snow who Tara was?" Logan asks.

I look around worriedly. I don't want to talk about anything in front of Milo. I pull Logan into an alcove with a wishing well. Thankfully, this one has a waterfall, which gives us some noise interference. I look around for mirrors. "Something weird happened my first day here that I still haven't told anyone about. A pigeon dropped a note at my window for a 'T.' It said 'T— She knows. Be careful. —R.' After Snow mentioned a Tara getting kicked out of RA, I started to think the note might have been for her, but there is no one I can ask to find out."

"It's not that big a kingdom," Logan says slowly, "but I don't know any royals named Tara." He scrunches up his face. "I wonder who she is."

"Me too," I admit. I think I can hear someone coming down the hallway. To be safe, I change the subject. "What class do you have now with the schedule change?"

"Some outdoor nature walk." Logan glances at his scheduling scroll. I do the same and see a news alert saying harpies have been spotted in the countryside stealing farmers' crops. The royal court is launching an investigation.

"What about you?" he asks.

Suddenly, a class update appears on my scroll. *GYM, 10 a.m. Physical activity to be determined.* That's strange. I'm not sure I have appropriate gym clothes in my locker. I should contact Brynn. "Apparently, I have gym now."

Logan makes a face. "Just as bad as my class. Good luck."

I've never really enjoyed gym class. While other girls at my village school enjoyed an afternoon of croquet or Billy Goats Bluff Ball, I would always rather leave school early and get out to the clearing to see my animal friends. I reach the gym and push the doors open. Inside the sweat-scented room, gray Royal Academy flags hang from the ceiling showcasing the tournaments and achievements won by RA over the years. The walls are covered with large RA logos painted with aspirational sayings. (SLAY NOW. ASK QUESTIONS LATER! says a picture of a fire-breathing dragon.) I don't see any students or our teachers.

"Hello?" I take a few more steps into the room. "Hel-*looo*? Where is every—"

A sack is pulled over my head as hands grab my ankles. Rope is wound around my hands and feet before I even have time to scream. After a few seconds of shock, I find my voice. "Let me go! Hey! *Hey!*" I shout as someone throws me over their shoulder.

"I've got this one! You get the next princess through the door," I hear someone say.

I can't see anything. All I hear is Lily hissing in my pocket. I swing my legs hard and hit my captor.

"*Ow!* This one is feisty!"

"Put her in the room with the others." We walk for what seems like a long time as I keep struggling before my captor stops and places me on the hard floor. I hear the footsteps walking away. Then sniffling.

"Hello?" I try to wriggle out of my sack. "Is someone else here?"

"Devin?" The sniffling stops. "Is that you? It's Raina! You're in this class today too?"

This is the most she's said to me in days (second only to "Did you touch my hairbrush?"). "Class? *Oh!* Class! This must be another test." I feel my body relax. I'm okay. It's just another of Olivina's trials. "Hold on. I think I can get my sack off my head." I wriggle like a snake for a few minutes before I succeed. I look around. I'm in a plain circular room with a group of princesses, including Sasha and Raina. Only a few girls have managed to get their sacks off so far. Sasha isn't one of them, but I can tell it's her by her silver lace-up boots.

"Don't worry, the princes will be here soon," says Matilda Locust, a girl in my How to Write a Love Note class. "The best thing we can do right now is sit calmly and wait. I wish we had a game to play." Matilda yawns with boredom.

I glance out the one small window in the room and see smoke and flames. *Nothing to be alarmed about. Just an illusion, I'm sure. This is just a test!* I remind myself.

"Maybe we should sing while we wait," suggests a girl who is sweating profusely. For fake flames, it is rather hot in here.

"I'd like my sack off," Raina says. "Can someone help me?"

"Let me try to help." I wiggle closer, then stop. Am I allowed to help Raina get out of her sack? Or is that against the princess rules? I look around for a mirror but see none. Does that mean Olivina can't see us? "Um…" My brow is beading with sweat.

"What is it? Can you reach me?" Raina asks.

"Yes, but…am I allowed to take your sack off?" I whisper.

"Of course you can!" Raina sounds somewhat annoyed. "I'd think Olivina would want us to look our best when the princes arrive, and I certainly can't do that with a sack on my head, now can I? Actually, let's all try to remove our sacks."

That makes sense. I inch closer and use my teeth to give her sack a tug. It pulls right off. The few girls with sacks off do the same for the girls around them. When someone reaches Sasha, I realize she's actually gagged as well. What is that about?

"There, that's better!" says Matilda, whose hair has started to wilt in the heat.

"I didn't realize magic could conjure up temperature as well as illusions," says another girl warily.

I hear a crackling sound and look up as a beam from the ceiling catches fire and plummets to the floor, narrowly missing Sasha's feet. A few girls scream.

"Fairy be, that's some illusion," Raina says nervously.

There's more crackling and… *Boom! Boom! Boom!* Three more beams hit the floor in quick succession, one cracking the floorboards. The entire room starts to rumble and shake, and black smoke pours through the window. Girls start to whimper.

"It's just a test, it's just a test, it's just a test," I hear a girl repeat over and over, and I do the same in my head. *It's just a test! But it feels so real! But it's just a test!*

Then I hear a low roar.

"That sounds like a dragon," a girl squeaks.

"No way!" says Matilda, shaking her head so vehemently her tiara flies off.

"It's definitely a dragon!" says the girl next to her. "It sounds like the one that was in Professor Snow's class."

"It's just an illusion," I say, but my words are drowned out by an earsplitting *ka-boom!* Pieces of the ceiling rain down on our heads as the roof is ripped away. Girls scream and huddle together, unable to do much more than press themselves against the wall with nowhere else to go. Raina and I stay close, but Sasha is clear across the room. I lock eyes with her. "It's going to be okay!" I shout as much to myself as to Sasha. "The princes are coming." The words sound hollow coming out of my mouth.

Screech!

A scaly arm works its way into the opening in the roof. The long talons that loom above us do not look friendly, but it's just an illusion. All smoke and mirrors.

Screech! The dragon looks down at the tower full of

princesses. *Maybe he can't see us*, I think. Then he spews a heavy stream of fire that licks the edges of the walls and sends girls rolling out of the line of fire. A table in the center of the room is engulfed in flames, blasting the room with blistering heat.

I lock eyes with Sasha and know, somehow, she's thinking the same thing I am: This doesn't feel like an illusion. This feels real.

"I don't think this is a test!" wails Matilda as the dragon begins ripping away more of the ceiling. "That dragon is going to eat us!"

"Where are the princes?" Raina cries. "Why isn't anyone coming to save us?"

My heart is beating out of my chest. Sasha scooches herself across the room so she's next to Raina and me. Tears are streaming down girls' cheeks. Some are crying quietly as the dragon caws and screeches above our heads.

"Those flames are real! This room is going to be destroyed in minutes. We can't wait any longer for boys to save us!" yells another princess. Some of the girls mutter in agreement.

"But that's what we're supposed to do," the girl next to her cries.

"We can't just sit here!" snaps the first girl. "We're like one hundredth to the throne. If the princes get here, they'll save the others first, and we'll be done for. We have to save ourselves."

"Ella is our stepsister! She wouldn't just leave us here," the first girl says and now I know why I recognize them. Azalea and Dahlia, Princess Ella's formerly wicked stepsisters, go here. (I hear it's on a technicality because Ella married into royalty, so her family isn't royal. I guess Ella has major pull with Olivina.)

"If she even knows we're here," the other sister says. "Remind me again why we didn't go to Fairy Tale Reform School with Mother? At least we'd be surrounded by villains there! There are no surprises."

Roar! The dragon drops onto a beam above us that sends the chandelier crashing down feet from the wicked stepsisters. Everyone screams. I wince, bracing for impact, then realize nothing's happened. I look up again. The opening isn't big enough for the dragon to get its head through. It flails around, trying unsuccessfully to widen the hole in the ceiling, then it lets out a frustrated roar and takes off.

"We have to get untied!" Azalea shouts, and I don't disagree. She looks at me. "You must know what to do. We heard you saved everyone in Professor Snow's room. How do we get out of here?"

The dragon's screech muffles my weak reply: "I can't." If I do, Olivina will expel me. "I…" I hesitate, unsure of how to explain myself.

The dragon screeches again, sending another round of fire that torches the wall next to us. The wall gives way, and I watch in horror as Matilda falls out of the tower, her screams echoing through the chamber.

"Matilda!" the other girls cry as the dragon flies off after her.

Raina and I look at each other. My heart is beating double time. Leaping dragons! I can't talk my way out of this with Olivina if I'm not alive to do it. Azalea is right. We can't just sit here. It's time for action.

"If one of us can get loose, we can untie the others." I think of the wildfire last fall when I had to help shepherd animal families to safety. "We just have to work together and fast. Girls, first get those wrists loose. Help each other! We can do this! Sasha?"

She starts mumbling frantically.

"We will get your gag off! Hang on!"

Girls go back to back, shimmying together and grabbing pieces of fallen glass or broken shards of wood to try to saw at their restraints. One by one, girls begin to break free. My restraints come loose, and I finally remove Sasha's gag and wrist binds.

"Thanks," she says, giving my hand a gentle squeeze.

"You're welcome," I say with a hesitant smile.

We hear a roar in the distance.

"We'll talk later, okay?" Sasha says, turning to Raina to loosen her restraints. I nod and join her.

Raina is just sitting there. "What did we do wrong?" she asks me, her face covered in ash. "The princes are supposed to come! Where are they?"

"I don't know," I admit. "But sometimes you can't wait for a prince to save the day. You have to save yourself, just like Red Riding Hood!" Girls stop sniffling and look at me. "We can get out of this tower on our own. We have no other choice."

"Okay." Raina sounds resolute. Calmer even. She breaks through her rope, then turns to the girl next to her.

Roar!

"The dragon," Azalea shouts, and girls begin to whimper. "It's coming back."

"We have to get out of here," Dahlia adds. "Now!"

I run to the window and look down. *Whoa.* We are so

high up that I can't even see the ground. How are we going to get down there? It's not like anyone has hair as long as Rapunzel's… *Wait.* I look at the loose restraints on the ground. "Everyone hand me their ropes!"

"Good thinking," Sasha says, running to me with hers. I quickly tie as many ropes together as I can, hearing the roars grow closer and closer. My hands are sweating from the heat and fear, and the rope pieces keep slipping as I try to tie them together.

"That rope is looking awfully short," Dahlia says with a frown. I look at what I've managed to cobble together so far, and my stomach swoops unpleasantly as I realize she's right.

"We just need more material…" I start to say, looking around for inspiration. I wipe my hands on my skirt and… *Wait, that's it!* I grab the side buttons and yank them apart, ripping my skirt off. The girls gasp.

"Your dress has pants under it!" Azalea says in awe.

"Purple polka-dot pants!" Dahlia adds. "How? Why? Who?"

"Marta sewed them into all my dresses," I say.

"I love them!" Azalea shouts.

"I want a pair!" Dahlia nods. Other girls start to chime in.

"Guys, we have to focus!" I say. "Right now, I need help

ripping the fabric into strips so we can lengthen the rope." In no time, the skirt is shredded, and we have a decent-length rope.

Boom! The dragon lands on what's left of the ceiling, and several girls start to shriek.

"Let's get out of here!" I shout as the ceiling hole grows bigger.

I see part of the floor start to buckle and could swear I see the tip of an ax poking through, but there is no time to wait. Azalea, Dahlia, and I help girl after girl shimmy down the rope. After Azalea goes, there are only three of us left. We're almost in the clear when the rest of the ceiling gives way. Wood, burning embers, and other debris rain down along with another burst of fire. This dragon is nothing like the one in Snow's classroom. It's angry, and it won't stop till it has us. His roar is so loud that I can't hear what Raina is yelling. I help Dahlia out the window just as the dragon begins to advance.

"Devin, come on!" Sasha shouts.

I grab the rope and start climbing down after her. I can hear shouting below me, and my heart is beating so fast, I feel like it might burst out of my chest. I'm covered in soot, and I could swear one of my boots is on fire, but I keep going lower, lower, lower, till my rope snaps back.

Holy harpies! The dragon has my rope in its teeth and is pulling me up.

"Drop!" Sasha shouts as she lets go of the rope and disappears into the smoke.

"Sasha!" I shout. I look down. I still can't see the ground, but if I get any higher, I'm going to be dragon brunch.

I take a deep breath, close my eyes, and do the only thing I can: let go. I fall through the air and brace for impact.

Boing!

I bounce off something supersoft and elastic like taffy. *Boing! Boing!*

"Grab her!" Sasha shouts. Hands extend toward me through the smoke, and I grab them. I've landed on some sort of giant bouncy substance. Sasha and Raina pull me toward them and into a…hug? I squeeze tightly back.

"I thought we lost you," Raina sobs. "I'm sorry I was so mad!"

"I'm sorry too," I tell her.

"We're alive!" someone shouts.

"So is Matilda!" I hear someone say as all the girls pile on to hug me. "Devin helped save us!"

I'm in the middle of a sniffling, laughing, huddle of

princesses, but before I can speak, the smoke starts to dissolve around us and the crumbling tower fades away.

Suddenly, we're looking at the gym again. A group of teachers and a gobsmacked Hazel slowly come into view, along with velvet-cloaked Olivina. My heart drops.

I somehow feel like I want to run and am going to faint at the same time. Olivina isn't smiling. In fact, she looks furious.

"Girls, that was another test," she starts to say, her voice pulsing with anger as she stares. "And you all just failed it." She points to Sasha, Raina, and me. "You three come with me."

WHO ARE YOU CALLING COMMON?

Poof! We land in a familiar room with floor-to-ceiling windows.

I feel my throat closing. *No, no, no.* I can't get another strike!

"We're in Olivina's private quarters!" Raina realizes, looking around. "No one comes up here unless they're being knighted, or crowned, or…or…are in trouble!" Her eyes widen, and she looks at me. "What did we do wrong?"

"Nothing," Sasha says somewhat defiantly, her eyes taking in the mirrors and the paperwork on Olivina's desk. "That fire was *real*, and if we hadn't saved ourselves, we'd all be burned to a crisp right now."

Raina relaxes. "You're right! We had no choice. The

princes never showed up. We can't get in trouble." She frowns. "I hope." Raina starts pacing nervously.

I sit down hard on an ottoman. "That was way too close a call, if you ask me," I say shakily.

"It's almost like she was trying to scare us," Sasha says, and we all look at each other. "Or to make us break the rules."

"Olivina wouldn't do that, would she?" Raina wonders.

Sasha walks over to where I'm seated and sits down next to me. "I'm sorry I blamed you for everything happening. I know you were just trying to protect us," she whispers. "But something weird is going on here, and until we figure out what that is, we have to play by the rules. Just act like you're sorry and scared, and say you'll do your best to be the perfect princess." She looks at Raina, who's still pacing. "Just act like Raina."

I nod worriedly. Something is going on here, but what?

Raina stops pacing to look at the wall where a dozen different scenes from inside the castle are on display. "Hey, what are all these mirrors showing? Is that our dorm sitting room?" A group of girls are sitting down for midmorning tea. Raina taps the mirror, and the volume in the frame increases.

"I give Devin a month," we hear Clarissa say. "Look what happened in Snow's class and at the first ball. A princess like that isn't meant to rule. Thankfully, we won't have to put up with her much longer." They all giggle.

"How rude! I really hope my brother doesn't pick that girl as his princess," Raina mumbles.

"Who cares what Miss Prissy thinks? Look at this!" I turn around and see Sasha is standing at Olivina's desk.

"I don't think we should be snooping around," I say nervously. Olivina could walk in at any moment.

The desk is covered in scrolls, various invitations, and a fruit basket with a note from Beauty and Prince Sebastian. Sasha holds up a piece of parchment, and her brow wrinkles. "This looks like a map, but I don't recognize the place it's showing." She holds it up for us and points to a large red circle. "Look at this. Someone wrote: 'T spotted again. This time on the western half of the woods. Not alone.'"

"Tara!" I gasp.

"Who is Tara?" Sasha asks sharply.

"Hey, I know a Tara." Raina walks over to look at the map. "Sasha, you met her too. It was at Rose's lake house two summers ago."

"Oh yeah!" Sasha says. "Wasn't she a first cousin of Harriett Abernathe? Or maybe it was a third?"

"I thought she said she was going to Royal Academy like us, but a year ahead." Raina frowns. "I haven't seen her here though."

"Where is she then?" Sasha demands.

The doors to Olivina's study begin to open, and we race back to the ottoman and sit down. Olivina strolls in and stops in front of us.

She uses her wand to pull forward a fuchsia-colored chair and sits down in it. "Now," she says calmly, folding her hands on her lap and lacing her fingers together. "Who wants to tell me what happened today?"

Everyone starts talking at once. Olivina holds up her hand, and we go silent.

"Girls, girls! It's not polite to talk over one another. You know that." Olivina's smile does not match her tone. "But I believe you were about to apologize for interfering with today's lesson plan. While I'm sure it wasn't your intention, consequences must still be faced. Students are already buzzing about what happened in your gym class."

"We thought we were going to die!" Raina bursts out sobbing. "My whole life flashed in front of my eyes, and all I could think was I've never had a coronation! I'll never wear a crown! Never greeted an adoring crowd of admirers! So when someone suggested we save ourselves, I did it because I was so scared!"

"I could *feel* those flames from the dragon," Sasha butts in. "We would have been princess s'mores if we had waited for the boys to come rescue us. We did the only thing we could think of."

Olivina dismisses my roommates with a wave of her hand. "You were never in any danger. The princes were going to make it there eventually. You all had your trials to face." Olivina sighs. "I don't understand what is going on with this new class at RA! So many rebels trying to twist the rules and do things a silly new way." She looks at me in particular. "Why mess with a system that works? I had everything under control as I always do."

"But…" I start to say.

She points her finger at us. "I'm giving you challenges that will prepare you for any obstacle! But as I explain over and over, there are rules and protocol that must be followed. No rescue mission is ever easy. No villain is ever predictable. If they were, then we wouldn't have to prepare ourselves, would we?" We shake our heads. "And if you can't handle a simple test here at Royal Academy, then what chance do you have in the real world?"

I want to point out that escaping the tower without the princes' help means we *can* handle stuff, but I know that's just going to get us in trouble.

"None?" Sasha asks hesitantly.

"None," Olivina agrees, nodding.

Raina's lip is quivering. "We're so sorry! We've failed you as princesses!"

I look at Sasha, who is dabbing at her eyes with a handkerchief. She gives me a meaningful look, and I know that's my cue to play along. I pull mine out and do the same. The next thing I know Olivina opens her arms and envelops us in a hug.

"There, there! One strike won't kill you. It will make you stronger! You won't mess up again, will you?" she coos.

"No!" Raina sobs. "I want to be on the superlative list! I promise never to think I can save myself again. A good princess waits for a prince."

I bite my tongue. Instead, Sasha and I just nod. The contrition act seems to be working.

"I know this is my second strike, but I've really learned

my lesson," Sasha says earnestly. "I won't let my foolish whims affect my decisions again."

"That's the spirit, Sasha! You're a smart girl. I know you mean that." Sasha nods. "My teachings have been effective for the past fifteen years. They're a proven system! I hate to think what would happen to you all if you didn't follow my methods in the fairy tale world. And I had such high hopes for you three. It's why I made you roommates!" We all start to talk over one another again. "Now, now! I can't hear myself think!" She scratches her chin. "I think it's time we examine what's steered you three off course." She looks at me pointedly. "It is my understanding that it was you, Devin, who led the princesses to climb out the tower window."

"I wasn't the one who suggested it," I insist nervously, and my roommates agree with me. The words *third strike* ring in my head. Am I about to be banished? I feel my breath start to come fast, and I hold my chest. "But I did help people out of the tower when I thought we were about to become toast."

"Still, your actions, once again, have affected our whole school's outlook," Olivina says. "When our most famous princesses' siblings can't follow school rules, how do you think that looks to everyone else?"

Before I can reply, the doors to her quarters open, and Hazel and Princess Ella come in arguing. I can't help trying to hear their conversation.

"I never ever wore pants, but I must admit they do look comfortable," Ella is saying.

"Pants are not comfortable! They're lazy and unfashionable! They're everything a princess is not," Hazel counters.

"But think of how wonderful they would be when out for a horseback ride or taking a Pegasus for a private moonlight flight." Ella blushes. "Sometimes I sneak out alone to do just that, and the wind makes wearing a skirt so...chilly."

Olivina is short. "Ladies, we were in the middle of a private discussion."

"Olivina, Princess Ella walked in after *the incident*." Hazel looks at me. "And we overheard princesses requesting appointments with Marta to have pants sewn into their skirts!" She glowers at me, and I find myself wishing my skirt wasn't in shreds back in the gym. I try to hide my purple pants with my arms.

"I don't see the harm," Ella says. "I see all the girls in the village wearing them."

"They're commoners," Hazel snips.

"I was a commoner before I became a princess," Ella tells her, and Hazel grows silent. "Pants would have made my chores so much more manageable."

Olivina is stone-faced. "I think that is enough discussion for one day. Sasha and Raina, you are dismissed. Hazel, I'd like you to contact Marta. No one is to have pants sewn into their gowns from this day forward." Hazel nods. "Now, I'd like to have a word with Devin."

"But—" Sasha interrupts.

"You will see your roommate later," Olivina says. "That is all." She waves her wand, and my roommates disappear. She turns to me, and her face darkens. "I had such high hopes for you and me. I had a vision of us working in tandem to change Enchantasia! I had heard you were a strong leader. Clearly, I was wrong. You are not the princess I thought you were."

"Am I getting a third strike? Am I banished?" I ask anxiously, hating how weak I sound.

"You're not banishing this student for failing a single test, are you?" Ella is horrified.

"She should." Hazel glares at me. "This isn't the first time she's stepped out of line."

Olivina strokes the fur on her collar, staring right at me.

I try not to crumble under her glaze. *Please don't. Please give me another shot.*

"Olivina?" Ella looks concerned. "We have the anniversary ball coming up. How would this look to our people? If word got out that we banished a student for such a small offense. Especially after what happened last year with T—"

"The anniversary ball!" Olivina cuts her off, her face brightening. "That's a splendid way for Ms. Nile to make up for her transgressions. Devin, if you join the student planning committee for the anniversary ball, I will keep you at two strikes."

Plan an anniversary ball? Not exactly my area of expertise, but as Sasha says, fake it till you make it. "I would be honored to join."

"Ooh, what a splendid idea!" Ella says. "The students always have such creative suggestions. The Great Pumpkin Coach Carving Contest they ran last All Saints' Eve was a huge hit with the kingdom." Ella looks at me hopefully. "We would love to have you on the committee. I'm the princess chairperson. Do you have any ideas you'd like to share right now? I know RA has been drumming up excitement for the event in the daily scroll briefings and through Hazel's announcements, so I'm sure you've hardly been able to think of much else."

Er…what has Hazel been saying in the announcements? I'm always late getting ready during them, so I rarely pay attention. Theme? No. Something about the ceremony? Maybe. An award Olivina is getting? I think so, but I don't know what it's for. But instead of coming up with a good idea, all I can think about is what will happen if I don't.

"*Any* suggestions?" Olivina asks me. "Surely you can think of a way to make your school shine. Clarissa has such engaging ideas. She really wants royals to be seen in a positive light."

Clarissa. Great. Think, Devin! You need to wow the fairy godmother! A way to make the school shine. If only Brynn were here, she'd probably have a million ideas. Brynn would make a much better royal than I would. She'd love to come to the ball. *Wait. That's it!* I look at Ella. If anyone will like this idea, it will be her. "What about inviting commoners? Professor Pierce says that ruling is about working in service to our subjects. Why not invite some of them to join our celebration as a symbol of what being royal is all about? We could run a contest, and the winners could be guests at the ball."

Hazel cuts in. "I don't think that's a very good—"

"I love it!" Ella says at the same time.

Olivina pauses, looking pensive. Suddenly, a smile begins

to spread across her face. "I like it too! Let's run Devin's contest and let everyone know our brilliant new student came up with the idea to open our gates to the world. If you're successful in your planning and I see you making a genuine effort, you will avoid a strike three. Do we have a deal?"

I think about my parents, my roommates, Brynn, and Logan—everything I'd lose if I were banished. I look Olivina straight in the eye and say, "Deal."

ROYAL ACADEMY

Royal Proclamation

Hear ye, hear ye! Let it be known that Royal Academy is running its first-ever contest to win an invitation to the upcoming Royal Academy Anniversary Ball, traditionally open only to royals. This year, thirty tickets will be available to commoners.

Interested parties should add their name and address to this proclamation. Winners will be chosen at random and notified one week before the event to give them ample time to find appropriate dress and transportation.

Good luck!

—the students of Royal Academy*

◇◇◇◇◇◇◇◇

This message has been approved by Headmistress Olivina.

PARTY PLANNER

If we can just hang that holly an inch or two higher, we will be all set. A little to the left. A little farther and…beautiful!"

I'm standing in the center of the Royal Academy grand ballroom putting the finishing touches on a banner I made entirely out of holly and winter flowers. I've enlisted a few hummingbirds to help me hang it. If you get close, you can see it's actually ivy curved into letters that spell out WEL-COME! Several chipmunks are busy scurrying along some of the ceiling beams, working with a flock of birds to weave a faux ceiling out of ivy. Normally, I'd be nervous someone would notice all my nonhuman helpers, which would lead to a lot of questions. But everyone is pretty wrapped up in their stuff right now, and no one's paying me much attention up here. Besides, animal friends are approved princess helpers. (I know this because I've finally started consulting the manual.)

All around the ballroom, princesses and princes are working on different activities. Some are directing ladies-in-waiting on how to make swans out of their napkins; some are making sure the china and the sterling-silver table settings gleam. Others are doing displays on the banquet serving tables or wrapping the night's parting gift (a small, glass Princess Ella–inspired pumpkin coach that's been etched by the town blacksmith).

I start climbing down the ladder I'm standing on, then pause, remembering Princess Rule 73: It's always good to make a prince feel needed. "Can someone help me down?" I ask the princes.

I put on a grateful smile when a blond-haired boy offers me his hand and leads me down the steps. "Thank you," I murmur. (Rule 27: A princess speaks softly and delicately in order to maintain a composed and regal appearance at all times.) "I'll be sure to save you a dance at the ball." He bows and walks away.

"Devin?" Clarissa walks up behind me with a clipboard. "Do you have the welcome sign completed?"

I try not to tense up. Our committee chair (*grr…*) would notice my stiff shoulders in this spaghetti-strap dress. There are no pants under this gown either. I put all those dresses in the back of my closet. Marta has been told not to fill orders for anyone who asks for pants, and I've been asked not to wear them. I miss them, but it's not all bad. You can hide a lot of things under a hoop skirt.

"I just finished, Clarissa," I reply politely, and the hummingbirds fly to my shoulder.

"Good." She crosses it off her list and looks at the birds. "I see you had help."

"A princess can always rely on animal friends for assistance," I say on autopilot. (Rule 31.)

"And what about the chair covers?" Clarissa asks. "Did you change the sash fabric from Little Bo Pink to Briar Rose?"

I smile tightly. "Yes. I just have to pick them up from the tailor."

Clarissa's smile matches my own. "Go now, or send your birds. I'd like the sashes done today. We only have a week till the ball, and I have a fitting that I need to get to. Have you heard? Heathcliff asked me to go with him."

"How lovely," I say pleasantly, even though the news

surprises me. Heathcliff and Clarissa? I thought he couldn't stay far enough away from her. What do I know? Everyone is acting a bit strange. Raina has thrown herself into after-school clubs. Logan has been going to allergy testing to find a cure for his dragon aversion, and Heath, well, he's started courting princesses rather than running from them. I guess that includes Clarissa. I heard the boys got a talking-to after the tower rescue debacle too. Something about failing in their duty to protect the princesses even though they all still insist the tower entrance was magically bolted shut so that they couldn't get in. Maybe I'm not the only one who's trying to play by the rules.

"I'm happy for you," I add. (Rule 42: A princess should always be gracious.) "You got exactly what you wanted."

"Didn't we all?" Clarissa says. "Now, those sashes. Let's not procrastinate. Princesses never do."

"Yes, Clarissa." I send the birds on their way and walk out of the ballroom and down the long hall that leads to the Royal Underground. I walk slowly, hoping by the time I return, Clarissa will be gone, but I don't complain out loud. (Rule 35.)

Milo follows me to each mirror I walk past, watching my every move as he has the past few weeks since Olivina and I had our little chat. I wish I could run away from him, but that's not going to happen in these new heels I'm wearing. (Rule 12: Footwear fit for a princess always involves a heel!)

Peck! I look up. That white pigeon is back. I've seen him a lot the last two weeks, but I don't dare go to the window to see what he wants. Olivina wouldn't want me getting distracted when there is a ball to plan. I keep walking. *Peck!* The bird flies to the next window I pass. Then a third. I turn to look at it finally, getting worried someone will notice me being followed by an animal and… *Whoosh!* I'm pulled through a door I didn't know existed.

"It's me!" Sasha whispers, holding up a candle. "I needed to talk to you somewhere we wouldn't be overheard."

"Milo will know I disappeared." I feel the rising panic and begin to feel my way along the wall to look for a way out.

"He'll just think he lost you. He won't think you were sucked into a wall," Sasha insists. "These tunnels are soundproof. I found directions on how to get into them under a floorboard in our room. Aren't they neat? Apparently, they were put in when the castle was built so people could go places unnoticed."

"Why would a new castle need that?" I ask.

Sasha's illuminated face lights up. "Exactly! *Why?* I need to know."

"I don't. I can't get in trouble again. You know that! I'll be banished."

"We aren't doing anything wrong," Sasha tells me. "And we weren't that day in the tower either. Devin, you and I both know that dragon was real."

I feel a burning feeling in my chest. "We can't go there," I tell her. "Even if we were able to figure out what's really going on, what could a couple of kids do about it? She's the most famous fairy godmother in the kingdom. We can't mess with her. Besides, she can see everything that's going on in the castle. She'd catch us and throw us out before we even made a move."

Sasha looks at me strangely. "Who are you, and what have you done with my roommate?"

I bristle at that and shoot back, "I'm doing what I have to. She threatened my parents, Sasha. What else can I do but fall in line or eventually find a way to convince her I should just go home quietly? You basically told me to do the same thing!"

Sasha looks away. "I was trying to protect you. I was

trying to protect all of us until I had something concrete on her, but I can't do this alone.

I step back. "I can't help you."

"Devin, you know she could have killed us with that test! And why on earth is she threatening your parents? My instincts tell me something is up with Olivina. I should have known from the second she threatened the *Enchantasia Insider*." She looks pensive. "Before that even… I've always thought there was something weird about all the power she has with the royal court. And at our first ball when she turned into a harpy? How did she get the other harpies into the school? My gut tells me something more is going on here. Do you know where she is right now?" I shake my head. "In the barn again. Every day this week she's been in and out of there for an hour, and it's not on her official schedule. What is she doing?"

I can't imagine Olivina going somewhere full of hay and horse poop. "I don't know."

"I think she's meeting with someone. But it's not a teacher, and it's not Hazel. She's usually standing watch at the entrance. She's hiding something. Someone needs to find out what's really going on."

She looks at me expectantly. Everything inside me says she's right. Sasha has two strikes just like I do, but she's willing to risk it all to get to the bottom of things. I'm not. This isn't the life I want to lead—ball gowns, waiting in towers for princes, or following princess rules—but I don't see a way out of it right now. Olivina is too powerful. I can't be involved in this, not when my family could be hurt if we're wrong.

"I'm sorry, I just can't risk it." I feel my way along the wall and hear a click. The door begins to open.

"Wait!" Sasha cries. "She's been harder on you than anyone. I really thought you'd want to help me figure out what's going on here. What if people's lives are at stake?"

"People's lives *are* at stake. Mine. My family's. I can't get involved. I'm sorry." I look at her sadly. "I'm trying to be a good princess now. It's the only way to keep everyone safe."

Sasha's mouth hangs open as I disappear through the crack in the wall. Then I pick up my dress, push back my shoulders, and focus my mind on the task I was asked to do: go get sashes.

Pegasus Postal Service

Flying Letters Since the Troll War!

FROM: Anastasia Hampton, lady-in-waiting at 7
    Cobblestone Creek, Enchantasia

TO: Devin Nile, Royal Academy

Devin, hi!

Thank you so much for the book, <u>Fairy Tales through the Ages: What We Can Learn from Them</u>. I've read it cover to cover twice!

I have exciting news! I won a ticket to the Royal Academy Anniversary Ball! I put my name down on the royal proclamation that was up in the village, and my name was chosen out of thousands! Can you believe it? I'm looking forward to seeing Royal Academy and meeting your friends. Is that okay? Are we allowed to speak to each other? No matter, I'll just be happy to be at RA!

Your original lady-in-waiting,

Anastasia

BEFORE THE STROKE OF MIDNIGHT

P resenting Princess Devinaria Nile of Cobblestone Creek," the crier bellows.

I stand at the top of the ballroom staircase and pause (per Hazel's instructions), listening to the applause of my classmates, the royal court, invited dignitaries, royals, and commoners.

This isn't you, a tiny voice reminds me.

I ignore it and smile, but I can't deny the moment feels hollow, as if I'm watching someone else play dress-up. I am comforted by the thought that Lily is with me in a hand-sewn pocket under my ivory silk skirt. I step forward, allowing the room to take in the majesty of my elegant gown. (Rule 93: Princesses must always make a grand entrance.) And I ignore how bad my head aches from the weight of the gold tiara on my head. Olivina sent it to me along with a note:

> *Great job keeping the fairy tale alive.*
> *Keep up the good work! —Olivina*

Sensing her eyes on me, I look over to the dais where she's sitting with the royal court. She nods approvingly, and I breathe a sigh of relief.

Next comes my escort, right on cue, looking dashing in a long gray jacket.

"Hey, friend," I say to Logan, speaking through my teeth, which are locked in a bright smile. (Rule 79: Never talk when being escorted into a gathering.) I hook my arm through his.

"Hello! You're looking very princess perfect," Logan whispers. "Shall we?"

Slowly, step by choreographed step, we descend the stairs in time with the music. As I look around the grand ballroom, I see all my little touches. From the slate-gray table linens to the ivy and flowers that drape the walls like curtains. Even the commemorative scroll that every guest will receive is something I worked on. It recounts a brief history of Royal Academy—how it came together, and how Olivina has risen to such great heights (Hazel dictated that part). I should feel proud, but instead, I feel sort of empty. I know party-planning skills are important for a princess (Rule 18), but who am I kidding? Choosing napkin colors just doesn't give me the same thrill I get from my creature care work.

Logan and I face each other when we reach the dance floor and begin to dance. I know we look good. We should after five private dance lessons. This committee and the ball have kept me so busy, I barely have had time to keep up with my coursework.

"Is your dress modeled after the one Rapunzel wore at her Get Locked Up for a Good Cause event?" Logan asks as he spins me past Heath and Clarissa, who is staring at my dress in awe. Raina and Sasha and their dates are also watching us from the edge of the dance floor, having already been introduced. Sasha and I have been coolly, quietly avoiding each other since that day she took me into the castle's hidden passages. "I saw it in *Happily Ever After Scrolls* last week."

"It is," I say, impressed he noticed. "She said I could copy

it after I donated two inches off my hair for her charity project. Like it?"

"Yes," he says, but his face clouds over slightly. "But it's
not very you."

I momentarily falter and stop dancing. If Logan can see
right through me, Olivina might too. I've been trying so hard
to fit in here, but it's so exhausting being someone I'm not.
"I know." I sigh deeply. "But what can I do? One more strike,
and I'm banished. I have to pretend."

"But you're better than... *Achoo!*" His eyes widen. "Why
am I sneezing?" He looks around. "Do you see any dragons?
Harpies? Villains?"

I glance around the room. Dwarf Police Squad members
are stationed at every exit. Hazel told us there would be heavy
security tonight, with the entire school and the royal court in
attendance. "No dragons," I promise.

"Good," Logan exhales.

"Devin!" someone shouts. "Devin!"

Anastasia, my lady-in-waiting from home, comes rushing toward me and pulls me into a hug. She smells like pine
needles mixed with floor cleaner, and suddenly I miss home
more than I ever have before.

I hug her tight. "It's so good to see you."

"You too! Your dress is beautiful," Anastasia gushes.

She looks lovely herself in a simple long red satin dress. "So is yours! Did you make this?" I ask.

"Yes, miss," she says with a faint blush. "I worked on it every night this week. I still can't believe I won. Your mother and father had hoped to come tonight, but your father was notified yesterday that he was being honored by Stone Harborton's Royal Navy for his bravery. He has never even been to Stone Harborton, but, as your mother says, 'Who are we to deny someone the chance to honor their favorite royal?'"

I wince at Mother's logic, but why would Father be honored by a province he's never been to? I try to shake off the feeling of foreboding and say, "Anastasia, I'd like to introduce you to my friend Logan. This is my original lady-in-waiting."

Anastasia curtsies. "It's a pleasure to meet you, sir." Logan kisses her hand, and Anastasia blushes. "Miss, I forgot! I have a note for you." She pulls a scrap of ivory paper out of her small satchel and hands it to me. "This carrier pigeon kept showing up at your bedroom window trying to get my attention. I still can't speak to animals as well as you do. Finally, he brought this note. It has your name on it."

Alarm bells are going off. Is this the same pigeon that's been following me? Who sent her? "Thank you, Anastasia." I slip the note into the top of my dress to read later.

"You can talk to animals?" Logan says in amazement. "Now it all makes sense! That's how you knew how to handle the dragon in Snow's class. Why didn't you tell me?"

Anastasia pales. "I didn't know you hadn't told him, miss. I'm so sorry."

"It's okay," I insist before turning to Logan apologetically. "I should have told you sooner, but I wasn't sure what you'd think."

"It's cool! You can tell the dragons to stay—*Achoo!*—away from me." We laugh.

"Hello!" Brynn appears out of nowhere, fluffing the bottom of my skirt and pushing a wayward curl behind my ear before extending her hand to Anastasia. "I'm Devin's current lady-in-waiting, Brynn. You must be Anastasia. It's so nice to meet you! I'd love to chat…especially about how you tame Devin's cowlick, but do you mind if I speak to Devin alone for a moment?"

"Of course," I say, surprised. Brynn has never asked to speak to me privately before.

"You two talk, and I'll give Anastasia a tour of the ballroom," Logan says, extending his arm to her and making her giggle.

Brynn's smile fades the minute Logan walks away. She looks like she might cry.

I touch her arm. "Are you okay?"

"Miss, I...I heard something funny. I'm not sure if I should say anything." Brynn looks at her feet. "It's not proper for a lady-in-waiting to gossip, but I know how worried you've been about your strikes and making a good impression with Olivina, so when I heard Hazel say your name..." She looks at me worriedly. "I got a strange feeling, miss, so I followed them."

The music is loud, thumping in time to my quickening heart, and people are dancing, so it's the perfect time to talk over the punch bowl. "What did you hear?" Brynn hesitates. "It's okay. You can tell me. I won't get you in trouble."

"I ran back to your room to get some more pins for your hair, miss," Brynn explains. "That's when I came upon Olivina and Hazel. I heard your name and hid behind a column. I know that's wrong." Her lower lip quivers, and I squeeze her hand.

"You were looking out for me. That's what friends do. What did they say?" I press.

"It was confusing, miss, but they were talking about a plan. A plan that would put *you* in your place." I drop Brynn's hand in surprise. "Hazel said something about someone making it through the barn like they'd hoped, and they'd tell everyone she came in with the commoners. They said it would teach you a lesson you wouldn't forget and that you'd be begging for forgiveness. You'd never step out of line again, they said." Her face crumples. "Especially if the witch takes your precious lady-in-waiting. Do they mean me?'"

"I think they mean Anastasia," I say, my fears and suspicions beginning to grow. I thought I'd learned my lesson. Isn't that why Olivina sent me this tiara? What is really going on?

"Ladies and gentlemen..." We hear Hazel's voice, and I jump. "Please give your full attention to our headmistress, Olivina."

Olivina stands at the podium in a beautiful pink gown and smiles. "Welcome, distinguished royals, students, and new guests! We are so delighted you could join us."

There is light applause.

"We hope you are enjoying your visit to our beloved

school and have met some of our fine students. They planned this lovely celebration. As such, I just received a note about dessert being served first!" She laughs. "Please be seated at your tables and enjoy the chocolate cream pie and banana pudding. I'm sure dinner will be served shortly after."

As everyone takes their seats, I'm gripped with fear. If Brynn is right, it sounds like Olivina is determined to kick me out no matter how hard I try to be the kind of princess she wants me to be. I'm the only one who knows something is going to happen tonight, and it's happening because of me. I can't let anyone get hurt, and I can't do this alone. I need help. "We need to tell our friends," I tell Brynn, and she nods.

"I'll find them," she whispers.

Five minutes later, Raina, Sasha, Logan, Anastasia, and Heath are staring at me across the table.

"What's so important you had to pull me away from Kensington Stevens?" Raina asks, her face dreamy. "He's the cutest prince here."

Heath shudders. "*That's* your prince pick? You could do better."

"So could you," Raina snaps. "Clarissa? Miss I-can't-talk-without-one-hand-on-my-hip?" The two start bickering.

"Hey!" Sasha bangs the table. "Why did you call us all over here?" she asks me. "Is this about Olivina?"

"Olivina?" Raina stops arguing. "What's going on with Olivina?"

I turn to Anastasia. "I need you to stay calm and listen. I think you're in danger."

"Miss, what's going on?" Anastasia asks, looking panicked.

"It might be nothing, but I need you to trust me," I say, taking her hands in mine. "Can you do that?"

She looks at me for a moment, then nods.

"Brynn is going to take you up to my room. As long as no one knows where you are, you should be safe."

"Be careful, miss," Brynn says. She takes Anastasia's hand, and the two ladies-in-waiting quickly excuse themselves.

"This isn't about dragons, is it?" Logan squeaks. I shake my head and look at Sasha.

"I think you might be right about her planning something," I say. "Brynn overheard her and Hazel talking about someone they planted in the barn and how they wanted to teach me a lesson. They said something about my lady-in-waiting too, which is why I sent both of them away. I don't want anyone getting hurt."

"The barn?" Logan panics. "Isn't that where the harpies were hiding?"

"Hold it together, Logan!" Raina snaps.

A server arrives with a tray of pie slices, but Sasha waves him away. "This explains why she keeps going to the barn! She must be hiding someone out there." She jumps up. "Let's go see what's out there."

Raina grabs her arm. "What? No! We're not going to leave the anniversary ball to poke around a barn because Devin's lady-in-waiting heard something she doesn't understand! Let's just go ask Olivina."

"No!" the rest of us shout. Including Heath.

I look at him curiously. "Hey, I'm in no rush to get back to my date. Plus, this place is a little obsessed with tradition. I'm all for ditching the party."

"I'm not! This is ridiculous," Raina is the most frantic I've ever seen her. "Olivina told us to come to her if we ever need her. That's what fairy godmothers are for." She stands up and turns toward the dais.

"Raina...wait!" I say, but my voice is drowned out by a

sudden popping sound. A huge plume of smoke billows from the middle of the dance floor. There are screams and shouts and running. I feel arms around me and realize Heath is dragging Raina and me back to the table, away from the mayhem. Logan and Sasha are already under the table skirt, watching the smoke clear. We duck down next to them and peer through the fabric. A woman in a hooded wool cape is waving a wand at the crowd and the royal court, who are huddled behind Olivina.

"Like my pretty desserts, my dearies?" Her voice is like sandpaper. "Good! Eat up! Eat up! Let's fatten you up for my stew!"

"Ewww! She wants to eat people?" Logan whispers. "I'm so glad I don't like chocolate cream pie. Now, if I had been back in culinary class and made you guys my mint chip soufflé, I guarantee you would have all devoured it."

"This is another one of Olivina's tests," argues Sasha. "She's trying to distract us. Let's just get to the barn."

"Are you sure?" Raina sounds alarmed. "I think that's the witch who tried to kill Hansel and Gretel!"

"Students!" Olivina cries as her magic wand is magically ripped from her hands. "Save yourself! This is not a test! This is not a—"

Boom!

Olivina passes out, hitting the floor hard, like a pancake. Students begin to scream and run again.

"Wait!" Heath tells us as Raina and Logan prepare to make a break for it.

Boom! Boom! Boom! The students around us barely move before they collapse like Olivina, their swords and tiaras rolling onto the ground. I look up at the dais and see the royal court is also fast asleep.

"A sleeping curse," Logan says. "She must have slipped a potion into the desserts. That never would have happened under my watch."

"So is this a test or not?" Sasha asks. "Who's the real one playing tricks? Olivina or the witch?"

The witch spins toward us, and I inhale sharply. Stringy black-and-white hair frames her pockmarked face, which is punctuated by a long jagged nose. How did a guest looking like that get past the Dwarf Squad?

"Look!" Heath motions to the witch again. "She's using Olivina's wand to steal everyone's jewels." Pearls, tiaras, diamond earrings, and other gems fly toward her and land in a big pile at her feet.

"Now, to pick a few tasty morsels to take with me along with this loot," she cackles.

"I don't think this is a test," I say. "That witch means business."

"But is she the person they brought in through the barn? It could be a trap," Sasha whispers as she crouches down next to me.

I feel a familiar rush, and my fingers tingle. Either way, I can't sit by and let people get hurt. If I'm right, Olivina can't get mad at me for saving her, can she? And if I'm wrong, well, I'll deal with that later. The words come bubbling to the surface. I can't stop them. "We need to stop the witch!"

Sasha nods. "I'm with you."

"So are we," Logan says, motioning to the others. "What's our plan?"

"We need to get Olivina's wand," Heath offers. "It's doing all of the witch's dirty work."

"How did she even get the wand to work?" Raina asks. "A fairy godmother's wand only works for the fairy godmother. It shouldn't be helping her steal."

We hear movement and lift the table skirt. The witch is moving through the crowd. She stops suddenly and cackles before she begins to drag two girls away. Wait a minute. I gasp. "Brynn and Anastasia!" They must have come back when they heard the witch. Anger consumes me.

"Devin, don't do anything..." Sasha warns.

I crawl out from under the table. "*Leave them alone!*" I shout.

"—rash," I hear Heath say as he runs up alongside me. "So much for having a plan. Guess we'll have to improvise. Hey, witch!" he shouts. "Forget the commoners! Want to take a prince with you? I bet I'd be quite tasty."

"Ew, gross!" says Raina, who I'm surprised to see has run up behind him. "Give us back that wand! It's not yours."

"Never!" the witch shouts, jumping over sleeping students and royals. "This spell won't last forever, and I need to collect as much bounty as I can while I still have time!" Sparks shoot out of her hands in our direction, and Logan and Sasha jump out of the way just before our table goes up in flames.

"We need that wand," I tell the others. I look at Heath. "Are you with me?"

He holds his hands out wide. "I've always liked a challenge. Let's see who can get it first."

We run at the witch from opposite directions, and she uses the wand to send us flying backward. I crash into an ice sculpture of Olivina. The sculpture falls from the table and breaks into smithereens. I get up slowly and see Raina waving her tiara in the air.

"Want this?" Raina shouts.

The witch runs toward Raina at full speed with the wand pointed directly at her heart. Heath dives at her from behind, knocking her to the ground, and the wand goes skittering across the floor. I run over and grab it, while Logan and Sasha help hold the witch down.

"No!" The witch reaches for it desperately. "Not the wand! It's mine! She said I could keep it!"

"Who did?" I look at Sasha.

"Give it back! Give it back!" The witch struggles to break free of Heath's grasp. Logan tries to hold her down, but the witch reaches up and bites him. Logan screams and lets go. I watch the witch make a run for it. She dashes across the floor, heading straight for my ladies-in-waiting. Anger consumes me.

"*No!*" I desperately aim the wand in her direction. "I won't let you hurt them!"

Poof! The witch dissolves into thin air. I drop the wand in shock.

"What in the name of Grimm just happened?" Sasha asks as people all around us begin to stir. "How did you do that?"

I back away from the wand in fear. That wand shouldn't have worked for me. This makes no sense.

"Devin! Raina! Sasha! My dear princesses, are you okay?" Olivina slowly sits up, looking very groggy. She falls backward again, and Raina catches her. "What happened?" she asks, looking horrified. "Was that the witch from Hansel and Gretel's tale?" The royal court awakens and heads straight for their fairy godmother, taking her from Raina.

"How did she get in here?" Olivina asks. "Is everyone okay? Why are there jewels all over the floor... *Oh*."

"She tried to steal from us," Ella says shakily. "She could have hurt the students. Or you!"

Olivina shakes her head. "This is why we can't leave our gates open to nonroyal guests," she says, sounding teary. Ella comforts her. Olivina looks at Snow. "I think it's for the best that our nonroyal guests leave. For their safety and ours."

Snow nods sadly. "Yes, Fairy Godmother. I'll see to it that everyone is escorted safely out the school gates."

My heart starts to thump wildly. A bad feeling is slowly

taking hold of me. I'm in trouble. I pull Sasha aside. "The commoners were my idea."

Sasha's eyes widen. "Then that means…she let a witch in to teach you a lesson? Brynn was right. You were set up. We have to get you out of here." Sasha grabs my arm. "We all need to find someplace to hide—and fast."

"We'll help you, Snow," Raina says, dragging Heath along with her.

I want to yell out to my friends that my initial gut feeling might have been right, but I can't. Anastasia and I make eye contact for a split second before the Dwarf Police Squad ushers her out. Someone puts their hand on my arm.

"Are you okay, Ms. Nile?"

I look up. Professor Pierce is looking at me intently.

"I'm fine," I say. "I just need air."

He nods, his smile kind. "You're going to be fine, Devin. You're a resourceful young lady. Everything is going to be okay."

Before I can ask what he means by that a group of commoners passes in between us, and the professor is gone.

"So good news, right?" Logan says, seeming happy. "The witch is gone, and Olivina seems fine. It wasn't a test. Brynn must have heard her wrong earlier."

I smile at Logan, not wanting to alarm him, but I think he's wrong. I look at Sasha. I know she's thinking what I'm thinking. A thousand thoughts cross my mind, and I try to figure out which ones I should pay attention to. The witch said *She promised I could keep the wand.* The *she* has to be Olivina. But why would Olivina have struck a bargain with a villain? Why does she want to put me in my place? Doesn't she want me to fit in? Nothing makes sense. All I know is I feel as though I'm in danger. And now my friends might be too.

The royal court helps Olivina step up to the podium. "My beloved royals and students," she says, sounding weak. "Tonight is a perfect example of why we cannot open our doors to just anyone. I know we want to be more accepting, but in these scary times, we can't allow royals to mingle with commoners. That witch came in here and tried to destroy us. The rules we have here, and the things I'm teaching you, are for your own protection. I hope you see that now."

"We do!" Clarissa sobs as Matilda blows her nose into a handkerchief.

"She's so right," I hear another princess say. "We can't let commoners in RA ever again."

"Commoners aren't the problem," Sasha says angrily

as the girls walk away. "Olivina is, and it's time the world knows." Logan and I look at her. "Look, I've been gathering information for a while, since before that sketchy dragon incident. With what happened tonight, I think I finally have enough evidence to expose her in the *Enchantasia Insider*. And with what Brynn heard tonight and everything we've seen happen here, I think we have an ironclad case against the fairy godmother: she's trying to control Enchantasia. We have to stop her. I think that's what the princess who lived in our room before us was trying to do before she disappeared."

"Tara?" I ask, and Sasha nods. I feel a flutter of hope in my stomach. "Do you really think it'll be enough to convince everyone?" I ask breathlessly.

Sasha nods firmly. "But she's not going to be happy about it. Devin, I think we're going to have to leave school before she can retaliate. I'll need to send word to my sister and have her talk to Snow as well. We're going to need backup. We have to get to the royal court first."

"Who is Tara?" Logan cries. "Sasha writes for the *Enchantasia Insider*? What's happening?"

"Sasha is going to stop Olivina, and we're going to break

out of Royal Academy," I say and throw my arms around him. Sasha does the same.

"Three cheers for Olivina!" a prince shouts. "Hip hip hooray! Hip hip hooray!"

The entire room echoes the chorus until they're so loud that the floor is shaking. The royal court is applauding, and everyone is cheering, including Sasha, Logan, and me, but for very different reasons.

Then, with a *poof,* we disappear.

NO LOOKING BACK

Poof! We land in Olivina's private quarters.

"What's going on? Where are we? Is this another test?" Logan panics.

Raina comes rushing over to help us up, and I'm so surprised that I fall back down. "What are you doing here?" I ask.

"I'm so sorry," she says hurriedly, her eyes wild. "I was only trying to help! I thought if Heath and I could tell Olivina what Brynn overheard, we could clear everything up."

I back away, shaking my head. I feel my heart tighten. *No. We were so close to getting out of here. To exposing her. But now Raina's exposed us first.*

"I wanted to defend you so you didn't get another strike.

I was trying to protect you! I didn't know she… I was trying to fix things." She starts to sob.

"Raina, what did you do?" Sasha whispers.

"She told me everything, of course," Olivina says, her face coming into the light. She has Heath held firmly by one arm. "A pity, really. She did the right thing. Well, the right thing for me, at least."

"I was just trying to help Snow," Heath tells me. "I didn't know we were headed here."

"Now Snow has no idea where her two darling siblings are, poor thing," Olivina tsks. "What will I be forced to tell her? How can I break it to her that her siblings went astray?"

"We didn't!" Raina cries. "I was trying to set things right."

"Isn't that what those in the wrong always say?" Olivina says with pity. "I'm sure Devin didn't think sharing what she learned about my conversation with Hazel would cause any harm to her friends, or that her actions in the tower would cause Ella to stand up against me. Just like Sasha didn't think I knew she was sneaking around trying to learn what I was up to." Olivina shakes her head. "If only you two could have kept your noses clean. Then poor Heath, Logan, and Raina wouldn't be in the same predicament you two are." Raina cries harder.

An uncomfortable feeling creeps over me, the same feeling I get when I sense danger in the woods. "This has always been about you, hasn't it? It's never been about what we need. It's about what we can do for you."

"I wanted you to learn to be a proper princess," Olivina insists. "That's my job!"

Sasha butts in. "No, you want us to be incapable of doing anything on our own. You don't let the princesses learn how to do anything for themselves, and you keep the princes busy with protecting the princesses. Then, when anything important happens, we only have one option... Wait for *your* help." Her eyes widen. "Help you give to royals when it suits you the most. Well, I'm not my sister. I don't just sit around and wait!" Sasha is shaking with fury. "You keep the royal court in line by making sure they always need you to help them make decisions. My sister thinks she can't function without you. That's how you always make sure you're the one who saves the day."

"You insolent children!" Olivina is fuming. "You know *nothing* about what it takes to run a kingdom. I *made* the royal court! Ella was a dirty little commoner, crying by the fireplace, before she met me. I lifted her up and helped her stop being so weak. Guided her on how to help her people and run a kingdom. I taught her everything she knows. And your sister," she spits out, turning to Heath and Raina. "She was so naive that she took a comb from a wicked old crone without a second thought. If it wasn't for me directing that witless prince, she'd still be asleep.

"And that's to say nothing of Princess Rose," she adds, sneering at Sasha. "But we all know how useless she is without me going into it. The royal court would be *nothing* without me. I pull the strings. I make the plays. Enchantasia is *mine*!" She clutches the back of a chair and pants with anger.

The five of us stand in complete shock, staring at the beloved fairy godmother.

"You're a puppet master, and we're the puppets," I say in realization. "What kind of school is this?"

Olivina sighs deeply and throws up her hands, then pulls a black wand out of her robe pocket. Her expression changes.

"Clever, clever children. I'm impressed you figured me out. I foresaw some of you having great power and being strong rulers." She glances my way. "I thought we could be allies, but you're just a bunch of meddling troublemakers. Even you, Raina! Running to me for everything! Well, now that you know the truth, I'll have to clean up your mess."

"You won't get away with this," I say, my voice barely more than a whisper.

Olivina's eyes flash. "Watch me." She begins to wave the wand in the air, and I know what's coming. There's nowhere to run.

"Wait! You can't just get rid of us!" Raina is frantic as Heath pushes her behind him. "My sister will wonder where we are. The royal court will send out a search party. They won't stop till they find us."

Olivina smiles wickedly. "I know. And who do you think they will trust to lead the search for a group of beloved first-year students?" Her face darkens into an evil smile. "Enjoy your banishment."

"*No!*" Raina shouts.

But it's too late. Olivina points her wand toward us and... *Poof!*

This time, I land hard on a patch of dirt. The world is dark and quiet, except for the soft rustling of leaves and the cry of a wolf in the distance. We must be in a forest. I reach in my skirt pocket and pull out Lily. She sticks out her tongue at me so I know she's thankfully fine.

Dizzily, I slowly sit up and see the others.

"This can't be happening!" Raina cries. "We've been banished!"

"Because of you!" Sasha shouts. "You had to run to Olivina behind our backs. We were going to expose her!"

"I was trying to save you!" Raina shouts.

"You were trying to save yourself!" Sasha argues.

"Now we're in the middle of nowhere, and Olivina is going to see to it that no one finds us." Logan pulls himself into a ball. "Except maybe—*Achoo!*—dragons!"

"How long have you all known Olivina is evil?" Heath cries. "Why did no one tell me?"

"Because you were too busy flirting with princesses!" Raina snaps.

As the group argues, Lily climbs up the front of my dress and plucks at the neckline. It takes me a minute to figure out what she's trying to tell me. Then I remember: the note Anastasia gave me! It seems like a lifetime ago that I stashed it down my front. I unroll it and look at the handwriting. It's familiar.

All is not lost. If anything, it's just the beginning. But to get through it, you need to be ready for anything.

This is Professor Pierce's handwriting. I'm sure of it! I remember it clearly from the magical chalkboard. It's nice advice, but what does it mean? And more importantly, did he know we'd get banished?

"Now we're alone in some spooky woods without food, water, or a sensible pair of shoes!" Raina is shouting. "No one will ever find us! She'll say a villain took us. She's made us outcasts!"

How do you stop the most powerful fairy godmother there ever was?

How do you prove she's actually evil and controlling everything we've ever known to be true in Enchantasia?

I look back at Professor Pierce's note. I guess we need to be ready for anything, whatever that means. It would be great to have some help though. Like from someone who's fought the system and won. Wait. *Ready for anything.* Where have I seen that phrase before? *I know!*

"Get up," I tell the others excitedly. "We have to get moving before the sun comes up. We don't want her to be able to see where we're going."

Sasha is the first standing. "Where are we going?"

The others gather around as I walk into the shadows of

the trees. The sunflower meadows shouldn't be too far a walk from here. I smile giddily, thinking of who I'm finally going to meet. My idol. "We're going to find Red Riding Hood."

ACKNOWLEDGMENTS

Kate Prosswimmer, you are the most willing, generous partner an author could ever ask for! I'm so thankful you embarked on this new journey with me and cannot imagine this story coming to life the way it did without your help. (Devin is lucky to have such a fierce middle name!)

Like the Royal Academy kids, I, too, am lucky to be part of an amazing team. Steve Geck, Kathryn Lynch, Beth Oleniczak, Margaret Coffee, Stephanie Graham, Stefani Sloma, Valerie Pierce, and Cassie Gutman—I've never met a group so dedicated to their authors and their books. Thank you for all you've done for my books. I'm also so grateful to have Michael Heath back to design another incredible fairy-tale book cover. I love how you've brought RA and Devin to life!

Aubrey Poole and Alex Yeadon, your touch is on everything fairy tale I do! Thanks for all your help along the way.

Daniel Mandel, thank you for being an incredible agent and sounding board. And three cheers for my amazing friends and family who are always there to offer advice and lend a helping hand: Kieran Scott, Elizabeth Eulberg, Courtney Sheinmel, Jennifer Smith, Katie Sise, Rose Brock, AnnMarie Gagliano, Lisa Gagliano, Joanie Cook, Elpida Argenziano, Christi Lennon, Marcy Miller, Kristen Marino, Lynn and Nick Calonita, and Nicole Neary.

On a fateful day this past December, I had the privilege of meeting Brynn Haun and her family when they visited New York. This incredibly strong fifteen-year-old graciously gave me permission to use her name in this series. Brynn is no longer with us, but I am honored her name will live on in these books, and I pray this character will do her memory justice.

To my family, Mike, Tyler, Dylan, Jack, and newest pirate/jedi Ben—home is only home because of all of you in it. Thank you for allowing me to do what I love every single day.

THE ADVENTURES CONTINUE IN

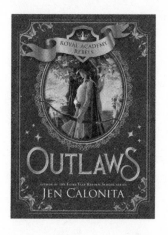

THE ACTION-PACKED SECOND BOOK IN THE ROYAL ACADEMY REBELS SERIES COMING OCTOBER 2019

Devin's not about to go down without a fight. Step one?
Find the famous Red Riding Hood and her vigilante friends
for backup. Step two? Come up with a plan to expose the
truth about Headmistress Olivina to all of Enchantasia…
or risk their homeland falling under villainous rule.

ROYAL ACADEMY

From the Desk of the Fairy Godmother

[URGENT!]

My Dear Students:

Sweet dreams should never be interrupted with sour news, but unfortunately, that is what I must deliver this morning. I regret to inform you all that several first-year students were expelled from Royal Academy overnight.

I know this information is hard to process. Many of us (myself included!) are still recovering from last night's attack on our anniversary ball. Thankfully, we have swiftly dealt with the security breach, and our school gates will be closed to nonroyals until further notice. The safety of you—my future leaders—is our top priority!

As for the first-years who were suspended, I know many of you will have questions, which is why I wanted to reach out before any vicious rumors started.

Students are only suspended from Royal Academy in the rarest of circumstances and only after committing three offenses at school. In the history of this distinguished academy, suspensions have only occurred a handful of times and only as a last resort. Unfortunately, try as I might, I could not get through to these wayward royals. It was decided their radical ideals were too dangerous to allow them to stay among our ranks.

For your reference, these students are:

Sasha Briarwood

Logan Nederlander

Devinaria Nile

Heathcliff White

Raina White

I know the pedigree of some of these individuals

is alarming—several of these students are siblings of members of the royal court—but the court backs this decision. It is heartbreaking to hear of royals who do not heed the call of duty, but ivy left untamed can overtake an entire castle. These students were attempting to change the way the world views royals and how we rule. In these uncertain times, why mess with a system that works beautifully? These students threatened this kingdom's very future with their lies.

Considering their offenses, there is to be *no* contact with the suspended individuals. If they attempt to contact you, your roommates, friends, or staff, or are seen anywhere near school grounds, call for me immediately. Failure to do so will result in *your* dismissal.

But don't despair! Follow the Royal Academy rules, remember your manners, and all your fairy-tale dreams are still sure to come true.

Forever yours in wishes,
Headmistress Olivina

◇◇◇◇◇◇◇◇

(For questions not answered here, please do not bother the headmistress. She is extremely busy! Contact her assistant, Hazel Crooksen, with any additional concerns. But truthfully, the headmistress answered all your questions already.)

THIS IS NO TIME TO PANIC

I used to daydream about spending my life wandering through the woods, helping animals in need, completely free of the responsibilities that come with being twelfth in line to the throne of Enchantasia. So you'd think being banished to a forest would be a dream come true. Expansive woodlands? Check. A plethora of wild creatures at my fingertips, just ready and waiting to be taken care of? Check. Stripped of my royal status? Check.

But if I've learned anything from my recent run-ins with a certain fairy godmother, it's "Be careful what you wish for."

Because as much as this situation seems like a dream come true, it's actually a nightmare. You see, a few hours ago, I kind of got me and my friends kicked out of Royal Academy and banished forever.

Banished as in we can't go home or see our families again.

Banished as in the whole of Enchantasia thinks we're criminal outlaws.

Headmistress Olivina dropped us in the middle of a spooky forest where the air is thick with dew and the trees cast such deep shadows I can't tell if it's night or day. The ground is wet from a recent rain, and we're surrounded by the sounds of a lonely wolf howling in the distance (I think it is crying about being lost from its pack, poor thing), an occasional low rumble of thunder, and sniffling.

My roommate, Raina, is not handling the banishment well. Snow White's younger sister is curled in a ball on a mound of leaves, holding her white gloves and crying. Her brother, Heath, is… Where is Heath? I don't see him anywhere. I can see our friend Logan picking edible berries for a possible breakfast. Logan may not be the outdoorsy type, but he knows how to whip up a meal even in the direst of circumstances. My other roommate, Sasha, Sleeping Beauty's little sister, is fiddling with the mini magical scroll she uses to run her blog to try to figure out our location.

Me? I feel dazed, confused, and quite frankly, angry. But I guess that's to be expected when your school's headmistress waves her wand and *poof*! Banishes you for not going along with her plans. Now the most beloved fairy godmother in Enchantasia is probably telling the kingdom we're a bunch of traitors when it's she who is the double-crossing, power-hungry villain.

"Drooping dragons, this is quite the mess we're in, Lily," I comment to my bearded dragon. That may sound odd, but she can understand me, just like I can understand her when she flicks her tongue at me in agreement. Communicating with animals is my gift.

Hey, that gift might be able to help us right now!

"Lily?" I call again to my lizard, who is camouflaging herself into the color of the tree trunk she's climbing. "Could you find a grasshopper or carpenter ant and ask if they know where we could find Little Red Riding Hood?"

"What?" Raina's response echoes through the early-morning air. She hobbles over to me wearing one shoe and carrying the other, which is missing a heel. Her dark-brown hair has several leaves in it, and her bow is sagging so much I'm sure it's going to fall off her head at any moment. I don't

dare tell her that. One's appearance is of the utmost importance to Raina (Princess Rule 2), even if she is banished.

"Are you seriously asking your *bearded dragon* to help us
find Little Red Riding Hood?"

She is pretty worked up, so I'm almost too afraid to reply.
I nod slightly to Lily, who hurries up the tree trunk and out
of sight before I respond. "Maybe?"

"That's how you're going to fix this...*situation* we're in?"
Raina can't even get herself to say the word *banished*. Her
eyes are wild. "By searching for a known outlaw to help us?"

"Red isn't an outlaw," I say, sputtering.

"She's as good as an outlaw!" Raina insists. "She was in the
same RA class as my sister until she left! We are not talking to
an outlaw, and we are not taking directions from a dragon!"

"*Bearded* dragon." Logan looks up from the berries he's
collecting. "There's a difference. Lily is a lizard, so she's not
a threat like a regular dragon. Devin trusts her instincts,
which means so do I. If we need to wait for Lily to find help,
we will."

I smile gratefully at him while Raina glares at the two
of us. Behind us, I can hear Sasha still angrily tapping at
her magical scroll ("Why won't you work?" she mumbles.

"Don't we have magic out here in the woods? What's with the bad reception?")

"I don't seem to be allergic to Lily either, which is an improvement, but..." Logan sniffs the air, and his nose wrinkles slightly. "I do feel a bit stuffy and light-headed." He touches his head and sits down on a nearby rock. "Maybe a real dragon is nearby. Lily?" he yells into the mist and low-lying fog. "Find Little Red Riding Hood fast! She's our only hope at getting out of these woods alive!" He claps a hand over his mouth. "Great. Now the dragon's heard us too. Why didn't I pay more attention in my seminar, A Prince's Guide to Surviving the Forest? Why?"

"It's *Red*. Not Little Red Riding Hood, and stop yelling!" Sasha drops her scroll on the ground in disgust.

She's woven her long blond hair into a makeshift bun with the use of a stick. Leave it to Sasha to pull herself together even in the most feared forest of Enchantasia.

"She hasn't been called 'Little' since the wolf tried to eat her," Sasha adds. "Doesn't anyone besides me read *Happily Ever After Scrolls*? She runs ads for Red's Ready for Anything Shoppe almost weekly. She's not an outlaw," she chastises Raina. "She just didn't want to rule her village! I even heard she's starting a store franchise. That means she isn't hanging out in a forest helping kids who've been banished for finding out their headmistress is a villain!"

Raina gets in her personal space. "Don't say such things! We don't know for certain Headmistress Olivina is evil, do we?"

Dear Raina. Always thinking the best of people, as a princess should. Logan and I are a bit more disenchanted at this point.

"We kind of do," I hear Logan say under his breath.

"Raina," Sasha says exasperatedly, hiking up the hem of her maroon dress. "Yes, we do know she's evil! Olivina knew we were on to her brainwashing ways, and she had us taken care of—and it's kind of your fault."

Raina's mouth forms a big, round O. "*My* fault?"

"Yes, your fault! You had to go and tattle on us for trying to figure out what she was up to!" Sasha's voice is rising in pitch. Logan is right. We definitely could wake a sleeping dragon.

"I was trying to save you all! You made a huge mess of things!" Raina shouts.

This could go on for a while. I look for Lily, but she's already headed off to talk to some locals.

"Girls! Calm down," Logan tries. "The truth is, it was both of your faults."

Oh, Logan. He's terrible at talking to princesses.

"I'm sorry?" Raina asks, but she doesn't *look* sorry.

"I was all excited to taste the roast duck with fig sauce I had suggested Chef make when, *poof!* Suddenly we're in Olivina's office learning she's the puppet master behind every fairy-tale story this kingdom has ever had—and she gets mad and sends us here." Logan rubs his stomach. "And now I'm hungry." He looks at his pile of berries. "I wonder what kind of tart I could make with these. If only I could start a fire and find a small pheasant to cook…"

"Fire?" I narrow my eyes at him. "I am not breaking up an animal family by roasting one of their members for dinner!"

Logan nods. "You're a vegetarian. I respect that. I might be able to make us a salad or a soup, then."

"How can you think about food at a time like this?" Raina moans.

"Yeah! I've got so many more important thoughts rattling around in my head." Sasha starts to pace and almost trips over a boulder. Her voice gets louder and louder. "How has Olivina gotten away with brainwashing students for so long?

What is she telling everyone at school about us? And how do we reach our families to tell them we're okay?"

"Hey!"

A handsome boy, a head taller than the rest of us, bursts through the trees. He's wearing a double-breasted ivory jacket with gold buttons, black pants, and shiny boots that are covered in mud.

"Where were you?" Raina sounds very unprincessy, but I guess that's allowed since Heath is her twin.

"Exploring!" Heath's blue peepers have been known to make girls pass out in the school hallways. "I walked about half a mile and climbed up a small hill that overlooked a stream. There are some caves nearby that would make a great camp till we get out of here. I doubt there are any banshees or giants in them this time of the year because it's too hot." He slaps a bothersome fly with a quick swat, and Lily crawls quickly back out of the brush to snag the tiny carcass. In the distance, we hear a crack of thunder.

"Hmm. Might be a storm brewing. Or it could be typhira? Who can say for sure? We should start hiking to shelter," Heath says.

"Did you say…typhira?" Logan stutters before sneezing

loudly. "I thought they were a myth! I definitely wouldn't want to run into one for real. They breathe fire and cause lightning storms!"

"I could swear I saw one once when I was scaling Mount Olivando." Heath shrugs. "I would have fought it off if I had to, but luckily it didn't bother us, so Father and I kept climbing."

Heath loves to mark off the places he's traveled on the fairy-tale map he had in his dorm room. His goal is to visit every kingdom in the land. He doesn't sit still, which is why Royal Academy wasn't the best fit for him either. For any of us, really. (Except Raina who lived for the place, so I do feel badly about her being stuck out here.)

"As I said, could be a storm." Heath looks up at the tree-tops. The canopy is so thick we can't even see the sky. "Either way, we should find cover."

"Hide in a cave?" Raina is shouting now. "Are you crazy, Brother? I spent months designing this dress with Marta Marigold. I am not ruining it hiking to a cave!" She holds up the bottom of her midnight-blue ball gown, which is weighing her down. I don't mention the hem is torn and covered in black mud. "What we *are* going to do is call for Olivina! Fairy godmothers come when called, right?" She looks around, her eyes wild. "She can poof us right out of here to the castle where we will sort this whole mess out. It's just a misunderstanding! We could never truly be banished, could we? We are future leaders. We need to go home. She'll let us go home. Right? Right? *Right?*"

Sasha and I make eye contact. The woods are making Raina hysterical. She needs a sedative. I wonder if there are any medicinal berries nearby. Or chamomile leaves that would settle her stomach.

"Raina, she's not letting us go back to RA," Heath says gently. "We're on our own. We have to find our own way, or find Red, like Devin said."

I hold up the note Professor Pierce gave me right before we met with Olivina. Lily reminded me I had it in my dress when we were banished here. The note Professor Pierce wrote is cryptic but the line "Be ready for anything" in the woods *has* to refer to Red. After all, her shop is called Red's Ready-for-Anything Shoppe. Professor Pierce wants us to find her. She's in the woods. I'm sure of it.

"Running back to Olivina is not going to get us anywhere," Sasha agrees. "She'll poof us somewhere remote next. Do you want to be sent to an arctic tundra run by the Ice

Queen? Or banished under the sea with a sea witch?" Raina looks away.

"It's like the time we were in the burning princess tower at school—the only way we were going to get out of there was on our own," I tell her.

"Exactly!" Sasha agrees, applauding. Heath gives a whistle.

"This is our chance to save ourselves and every royal at that school who doesn't know how wicked the fairy godmother truly is." I stand up on a small rock, feeling empowered by my own words. It's as if I can hear the music crescendo in my head. Raina is staring at me now. I must be getting through to her.

"Red is here in these woods. Professor Pierce is trying to help us."

"Yes!" Logan agrees.

"I can feel it, just like I can feel an owl who is crying out for eye drops. Don't you see? Red must know how to help us stop Olivina! We're going to get the help we need to take her down and make our own future! Now who's with me?" I raise my right fist into the air, lose my balance, and slip off the mossy rock, landing in… Oh my. What is that smell?

"Uh, Devin, I think you fell in a pile of dung," Logan starts to giggle.

Heath joins him, and so does Sasha. Finally, Raina can't help herself. As I pull myself out of the smelly muck, I can't help but let go and laugh at the absurdity of it all too.

Until a package falls from the sky and hits Logan in the head.

ANYWHERE BUT HERE

Logan goes down like a tree in a major storm. Lily scrambles onto his chest and flicks her tongue at his face as a book lands next to him, narrowly missing his right ear. We all run to his side.

"What just happened? Am I still in the forest? Did a typhira get me?" Logan's eyes are dazed.

"No, you got hit in the head by a package." Heath helps him sit up as Sasha unwraps the box. There is a scroll inside. "I think you'll live."

A dove flutters to the ground next to me and coos in my direction.

"Demetris!" I extend my arm so the dove can climb onto it. "How did you find us?"

Brynn Haun sent me, Demetris tweets.

"Brynn?" I am startled by the mention of my Royal Academy lady-in-waiting. Brynn may have been the second-to-last girl to be picked for a position at RA, but in my book, she's aces. She may not have a title, but she carries herself way more regally than I ever will. She's also back at Royal Academy with Olivina, which makes me nervous. What if Olivina has it in for her because of me? "Drooping dragons, is she okay?"

She's fine, miss! Demetris says. *She's getting reassigned in your absence.*

I clutch my chest. "Thank the fairies."

"I can't get used to this 'talking to animals' thing she's doing," Heath mutters.

"Snow White talks to animals all the time," Sasha reminds him.

Demetris continues to twitter. *She wrote you a note, miss, explaining everything. She said to make sure you got that book too.*

Demetris's breathing seems a bit labored. That was a heavy load for him to carry.

"Heath, can you fetch Demetris some fresh water?" I ask. "And Lily? Go find Demetris a juicy worm or two. He must be exhausted from his journey."

I am, miss! But Brynn said getting you that package was of the utmost importance. I couldn't be seen so I came in the dark.

I stroke the bird's back. "Thank you, friend." I unroll the parchment and find not one, but two papers inside. One is a declaration from Headmistress Olivina. Just seeing her signature on the bottom of the page makes me feel as ill as a squirrel who ate too many nuts before the winter season. I read the scroll quickly and am not surprised to learn Olivina banned students at RA from communicating with us. We are officially outcasts. Grimly, I pass the note to Heath who shows it to the others. Raina audibly gasps as she reads it. Next, I open the note from Brynn.

Miss,

I hope Demetris finds you! When the scroll from the headmistress arrived in the ladies-in-waiting quarters, I feared the worst. I don't understand your banishment, miss! Most of the students (other than then wretched Clarissa) don't either! But instead of crying, I decided to practice Princess Rule 43: "Never let the world see through your mask! A princess always looks happy and ready to face whatever challenge is at hand!" (I marked the page for you.) So instead, I went to your quarters to gather some of your important things.

Alas, I was too late. The headmistress must have sent someone in there already, because everything was gone. I regret not getting your animal care kit out in time.

She seems mighty angry, miss, and while her proclamation tells the students to steer clear of you all, I fear she won't do the same. She's been calling for things from her quarters all night, and Ms. Crooksen has been frantically running up and down the halls. She's afraid of something, miss, and I can't figure out what it is, but I know it must have to do with you. Please stay hidden until I can learn more about what's going on.

In the meantime, I got a copy of the Royal Academy Rules book for you. Just because you aren't at school doesn't mean you can't stay polished!

Stay safe!

Your lady-in-waiting,

Brynn

I hand Brynn's note to Sasha while Raina grabs the book and holds it to her chest. "The *Royal Academy Rules*! Thank the fairies we have something civilized to read out here!" I can hear her mumbling rules to herself as she walks off. (Princess Rule 15: When you can't find a polite way to say goodbye, don't say goodbye at all. Allow someone else to offer your regrets for you.)

"That should keep my sister calm for a while," Heath says. "Until she remembers she's still banished."

"Princess Rule 22!" we hear Raina recite from nearby. "'You can never pack too much for a journey. Will your final destination be balmy or breezy? Weather is unpredictable, so you should always be prepared for any type of—' *Ahhh!*"

Raina's high-pitched scream sends a swarm of bats flying out of a nearby tree, causing Logan to drop back down to the ground. The rest of us go running toward the sound of Raina's voice. I push my way past the trees Raina just disappeared into and find…nothing.

"Raina?" I swat away a few lingering bats (*What's all the ruckus?* I hear them screeching) as Sasha echoes my call. "Where are you?"

Heath shushes us. "Stop shouting. You'll give away our location."

"To whom?" Logan's voice wavers.

"Anyone!" Heath uses a large stick to swat large palm branches in our path. I follow his example by grabbing a large branch from the ground and doing the same. "We should stay out of sight till we figure out our next move. What if Olivina is watching us?"

Logan and I stare at the skyline worriedly.

"But how are we going to clear our names if we're stuck in a forest without any mini magical scrolls or Pegasus Post?" Sasha asks. "We'll have no chance to—*Aaah!*" She vanishes into thin air.

"Sasha!" I scream, racing to the spot she was standing in, but she's already gone. Dead leaves crunch beneath my feet as I spin around searching for a clue as to what just happened.

I notice Heath pulling Logan back. His eyes are wide in terror. "Devin, you need to move. Walk slowly backward, retracing your steps toward us. Now!"

I know Heath is trying to act all macho and in charge out here, but I know what I'm doing too. I step forward, mid–eye roll. "Heath, what are you—"

The ground disappears beneath my feet, and my body free-falls. My scream gets lost somewhere in the darkness.

ABOUT THE AUTHOR

Jen Calonita has interviewed everyone from Reese Witherspoon to Justin Timberlake, but the only person she's ever wanted to trade places with is Disney's Cinderella. When Jen isn't plotting, she's working on stories in the Fairy Tale Reform School series and in her new

© APRIL MERSINGER PHOTOGRAPHY

Royal Academy Rebels series. She lives in Merrick, New York, with her husband, two sons, and their Chihuahuas. Visit Jen at jencalonitaonline.com.